WOMEN
WHO
LOVE
&
OTHER
STORIES

Cover design by Leif Sodergren

ISBN 978-91-979188-7-9

LEMONGULCHBOOKS
www.lemongulchbooks.com

To the memory of
my very dear friend, Lise Roche Bragg
who in Oxford long ago told me she
could pluck music from the air
with her Oxfam fan --
and she did.

Also by Donovan O'Malley

LEMON GULCH
New Edition of the
Comic Cult Classic.

THE IMPORTANCE
OF HAVING SPUNK
A Comic Novel with a twist
to the battle of the sexes,
and a nod to Oscar Wilde.

OUR YANK
An American student comes
of age in Oxford during the
Cuban Missile Crisis of 1962

THE FANTASTICAL MYSTERY
OF RITTERHOUSE FAY
A London Tale

THE JIMMY JONES SKANDAL
A humorous bedtime story
for grown-ups.
Illustrated by the author

WOMEN
WHO LOVE
&
OTHER
STORIES

DONOVAN O'MALLEY

CONTENTS

WOMEN WHO LOVE

Peggy burst through the door, kicked off her black heels, cast aside her black coat, black hat and handbag and flung herself into the nearest chair -- his reading chair. He wouldn't be using it anymore. Not today, not tomorrow, not ever! Willy got what he deserved!

Peggy, dazed, crouched for a moment in Willy's surprisingly comfortable chair. She'd never been allowed there whilst the lord and master was intact. Well, not really, but... She blew her nose into a black lace hanky. Her despotic friend, Jean, had ordained she wear only black, hankies included. Jean, bless her overbearing heart, had managed the whole pompous affair! Damn Jean! Damn Willy! Oh, if Jean could only see her now. Peggy tore off her fine, black, chosen-by-Jean-dress and flung it at the study door, his study door, Willy's study door -- forget your books, Willy, forget your pipes and your stinking tobacco and your goddamned Sibelius! You'll not be using them again either!

Jean had driven her home, threatened to come in and make her a cup of tea -- to soothe her and paw her with those thin black-gloved fingers and strike some absurdly sentimental pose. Peggy frowned and blew her nose savagely into the despised black lace hanky. She might have laughed had she not been so angry. "Damn it!" she cried and rushed into the kitchen, grabbed a kettle and slammed it on the cooker, flicked on the gas and leant smiling over the small, blue ring of fire -- smiling at how Jean had so wanted to be let in to bore her to tears. But was denied entry!

Margaret too, had pleaded to come home with Peggy and

commiserate. But Margaret was, as always, too stupefyingly drunk for even the most sedentary commiseration. Margaret, poor cow, who could scarcely remain upright for two hours together, considered herself a born empathizer and intended to practise it forthwith. This was assuming that Peggy would allow her into the house, which Peggy had no intention of doing -- ever. Margaret knew why.

Peggy cried out as the telephone rang and swore as she tore her slip on the study door latch, stood for a moment idly pulling at the tear. The telephone continued to ring. She tried to ignore it but was soon drawn and found herself in Willy's study standing over his telephone as it clanged monotonously again and again. She shook herself suddenly, comically, as a dog might shake off water, made a face and dropped into Willy's desk chair and picked up the phone. She didn't speak, only breathed heavily into the receiver. She knew it would be Margaret.

"Who is this?" slurred Margaret. "Peggy? Peggy, are you there?"

After a moment Peggy managed "I'm here."

"Are you all right?"

"I'm all right," said Peggy.

"Are you sure?"

"I'm sure."

"You sound strange."

"So do you. Are you sober?"

Margaret ignored this and pressed on, carefully pronouncing each word to deflect Peggy's unnecessary, cruel allegation. How could she be anything but sober on such a day?! *His* funeral! "Are you sure you are all right?"

"I am sure I am all right," said Peggy, miming Margaret.

"You don't *sound* all right," said Margaret.

"Well, I am."

"You don't *sound* all right," repeated Margaret. Peggy was silent.

"Peggy?" said Margaret, alarmed.

Peggy remained silent.

"I'm coming over!" cried Margaret.

"You are not coming over."

"I am!"

"I won't let you in."

"Yes you will!"

"No, I won't."

"Yes you will. I should have come directly home with you. Peggy, are you certain you're all right?"

Silence.

"You're not playing those horrid little tape cassettes, are you?"

Peggy was silent.

"Those horrid little cassettes?"

Peggy was silent.

"It's not healthy, listening to those horrid cassettes. Willy's gone and there is absolutely nothing you can do about it," said Margaret, "Nothing." Then, after a moment: "Absolutely nothing!"

"I shall be the judge of that, you nattering... bitch!"

"That was cruel, Peggy," moaned Margaret into her telephone as she stared at her white-knuckled grip on the large glass of whisky in her left hand. "Are you sure you're all right?"

"I am all right!"

"You don't sound all right. I'm coming over!" cried Margaret.

"I will not let you in!"

Peggy's kettle had been whistling for several minutes.

"My kettle's boiling," said Peggy.

"I'm coming over!" cried Margaret. "We'll have tea. I can make you a nice cup of tea. What do you think of that?"

"Not much. My kettle calls. Toodle-loo!" said Peggy, slamming down the telephone. She stared for a moment at the receiver still quivering in its cradle and went to the kitchen and poured boiling water into the teapot. She swirled it round to warm the pot and dashed the water into the sink, measured in tea-leaves from an ornate tea tin and filled the teapot. By habit she took two cups and saucers from the cupboard and set them on a tray. She paused for a moment and removed one cup and saucer from the tray and, meaning to return them to the cupboard, dropped the cup which shattered on the tiled sideboard. She ignored the broken cup, put out a tiny pitcher of milk, and placed a tea-cosy over the teapot and carried the tray into the study where she set it on Willy's desk. She dropped herself again into his desk chair and pulled out a drawer from which she removed a revolver, Willy's revolver. She clicked open its chamber and a few bullets fell on the desk, rolled and clattered to the floor. She kneeled and retrieved them, began to place them carefully back into the revolver's chamber and jumped as the telephone rang. She gazed dully at it as it rang several times. At last she lifted the receiver, restrained herself, said "Hello."

"Oh. You're speaking now," said Margaret triumphantly.

Peggy was silent.

"You sound better."

Peggy managed a tiny, ironical laugh.

"Much better. You're sounding so much better. John Lennon was shot today. I just heard it on the radio. He's dead. Dead as a doornail."

"Aren't we all?" said Peggy. "Goodbye, I'm going to the loo."

"What are you going to do in the loo?!"

"Pee."

"Stay away from Willy's razor!"

"I do not pee on razors."

"If I come over will you let me in?"

"No." Peggy heard Margaret's glass clink as Margaret swallowed and set it down.

"You're a cow. I'm coming over anyway," insisted Margaret.

"So be it. But be warned. I will not let you in."

"You've been listening to those horrid cassettes, haven't you? It's unhealthy. It's inappropriate to listen to lies at a crucial time like this."

"Got to pee. Bye-Bye." Peggy put down the telephone and poured a cup of tea, added milk, stirred and took a careful sip, too hot just yet. She leaned back in Willy's desk chair and gazed round the room. His room. The study -- Willy's room. Her eyes were caught first by Willy's pipe stand, then a very old framed photo of her deceased but nevertheless excruciatingly handsome young husband on the desk. On the wall behind was Willy's tastefully framed medical certificate. She turned. Along the opposite wall was a bookshelf of Willy's medical books that she, inveterate reader that she was, had never touched. They were medical books weren't they? She was a Henry James reader in any case -- James and his ilk, and should never have felt at all guilty -- but she did -- felt guilty that she hadn't taken the slightest interest in Willy's Medicine -- besides, of course, putting Willy through Medical school by the sweat, well not really, the sweat of her brow -- she had been a local librarian. Of course, she also had a not so small annuity which was *such* a help. Do local librarian's brows sweat? Hers didn't. But perhaps other local librarians brows did sweat. Willy would know. Particularly if that other local librarian was a woman. Particularly if that other woman was drop-dead gorgeous. Yes. Willy would know. But Willy wasn't here. Sad, that. For Willy. And that was it, for now. For today, next week, for always. Question time is over children. Forever. Class dismissed.

Peggy's gaze was caught by a gleam on the rug at her feet, a stray bullet from Willy's revolver. She stooped and snatched it up it and found herself peering directly into the open top of Willy's fine old phonograph. The record on its turntable was that late, Sibelius symphony which Peggy couldn't bear to hear ever again. He'd teased her that awful night, just before... She hated that particular symphony but Willy, who was a terrible tease, played it constantly. She liked most of the other records in his collection. She loved the Ravel and the Scarlatti and the Mozart -- even, very occasionally, the Wagner. But the Sibelius...

She rose, swelling with an odd, angry bravado, marched to the kitchen and got a large carving knife from a drawer and returned, slashing the knife before her in the air. She kneeled, switched on the phonograph and as the record revolved she raked her knife across it. She was shaking as she threw herself into Willy's desk chair, tossed the knife on the floor. She took a sip of tea and whispered "Fuck!" as the telephone rang. She stared at it, held her breath as it rang again and again. It stopped, and relieved, she breathed out. But it began again and continued to ring till Peggy set down her tea and screamed "Hello!"

"Hello, dear, Jean here."

"Hello, Jean," said Peggy-of-ice.

"Well," said Jean, "I only rang, dear, to --"

"Thank you," said Peggy, cutting her off.

"Is there anything..." continued Jean uncertainly, "Well... is there anything I can --"

"No," said Peggy, again stopping Jean mid-sentence.

"Well. I thought you might come and stay with Jack and me for a few days" said Jean, reasonably, "Just until things settle down."

"What things might they be?"

"Well...welllll..."

"A well is a hole in the ground," muttered Peggy. "How very kind of you but I'm visiting an aunt of Willy's for a few days."

"Oh?"

"For a few days. She's become unhinged since Willy snuffed it."

Jean gasped, said "When you come back we'll have lunch."

Jean was relieved and Peggy knew it, sang "Splendid!"

"Good. Well, that's settled."

"G'byee!" warbled Peggy, "Thanks for ringin'."

"Goodbye, dear. I'll see you when you --"

But Peggy had hung up and was now holding the muzzle of Willy's revolver to her head, thinking what a fuckingly silly thing it was to do.

Early that evening, Peggy, in her torn slip lay motionless in Willy's reading chair as Margaret pounded frantically at the door, crying "Peggy! Answer me! Peggy! Are you all right?"

"Go away!" shouted Peggy after several minutes during which Margaret became increasingly hysterical.

"Thank God you're all right!"

"Go away!"

"You are not well!" screamed Margaret, "I will not go away!"

"I will not let you in!" shouted Peggy.

"I have walked all the way from Victoria bloody station! You will let me in!"

"Piss of!"

"No!"

Margaret's shadow lurched across the window curtains and she peered through a gap between them. "You're in your slip. You'll catch cold. Let me in!"

"You slept with Willy!" cried Peggy. "Damn you!"

"I did no such thing! Let me in!"

"Climb in the window!"

"I shall!"

Peggy jumped up, ran to the study, grabbed Willy's revolver from the floor and crammed it into its desk drawer. She took a broom from a cupboard, rushed to the window and began to swat Margaret's hand which had come in through a narrow gap and was attempting to open it wider.

"You shall not!" cried Peggy with each swat of the broom on Margaret's flailing fingers.

"Shall!" screamed Margaret as she attempted to fend off Peggy's ever more energized swats.

"Shall not!" screamed Peggy.

"Brute!" screamed Margaret.

"Go away! I want Willy to myself today!"

"I knew it! You've been at those horrid, lying cassettes, haven't you? Watching those horrid old home movies. They're lies, Peggy! And you know it!"

"Go away, Mar-gar-et!"

"I'm Maggie! Do not call me Margaret! It's unfriendly! Those cassettes, those home movies! Jean said you'd be watching them! It's sick! Willy's gone! Jean said..."

"Jean said, did she?"

"Yes! Jean said!"

"You slept with Willy! Damn you!"

"It meant nothing!"

"Nothing to Willy! Everything to you! God! That day in the garden. I'll never forget that wretched day at our garden party."

"You've a nasty memory, Peggy. It does not serve you well. That was years ago."

"You pretended to have diarrhea!"

"I was not pretending!"

"You spent a half hour with Willy in the upstairs loo."

"*On* the upstairs loo! Your nasty memory does not serve you well."

"Thirty minutes in the upstairs loo with Dr Willy. You feigned diarrhea."

"It was diarrhea! Caused by your treacherous salmon mousse!"

"She poops to conquer!"

"Don't be vulgar!"

"You lured him into the upstairs loo with your phony grunts and spurious squeaks. You pretended to poop to conquer my Willy!"

"He was my Willy! I met him first! He was my Willy! He was never your Willy!"

"He was anybody's fucking Willy!" cried Peggy.

Peggy stood limp, numb, taking in what she had said. She calmly replaced the broom in its cupboard, flicked on the door light and said "Go away now...Maggie."

Margaret, who had moved from the window, now hunched on a stone ledge in the tiny entry garden and began to sob. "Peggy, I miss him so!"

"Please, Maggie," said Peggy softly through the window "Please go away."

"What? What did you say? I can't hear you."

"I'm going to stay with Willy's aunt. I'll ring you when I come back."

"What aunt? Willy didn't have any aunts," sniffled Margaret.

"In Yorkshire. She's nine-nine. Willy's death has unhinged her. I'll ring you when I return. We'll have lunch."

Margaret took a large hanky from a stylish handbag and blew her nose. "What did you say?" she sniffled. "It's difficult carrying on a conversation with a wall."

"We'll have lunch when I get back from Yorkshire!" shouted Peggy from the window.

"Willy didn't have any aunts -- promise you'll ring? Promise?"

"Promise."

"Liar. You're very cruel, Peggy." Margaret blew her nose. "I'll leave if you promise."

"I have promised."

"Willy and me. It was a long time ago," said Margaret. "And you know it. You have always known it."

"I know I know it, Maggie."

"It was years ago. I hardly remember it," said Margaret.

"Understandably," shot back Peggy, "You were sozzled in the loo the first time, drunk out of your mind the subsequent umpteen times and completely unconscious the rest."

"Liar! I was none of these dreadful things you...you suggest!" cried Margaret.

"Not a suggestion, darling. Hard fucking facts."

"Your memory serves you badly. It is not becoming. Nor is your language."

"Look. Go. I'll ring you. When I get back."

"I could have given Willy a child!" bawled Margaret through a harsh burst of tears.

"You weren't the only one in Willy's queue!" cried Peggy through the window.

"You're a cow for not letting me in. I could have used a nice, hot cuppa. You're a cow."

"When wasn't I a cow?"

Margaret rose unsteadily from her perch on the stone ledge. "It's cold, Peggy. I'll probably get horrid piles from sitting here on that hard, cold rock."

"Better than diarrhea though, ain't it? Better than diarrhea in the upstairs loo!"

"No! No, it *ain't!* And I'm cold!"

"Have a drink, Mags! You've surely got a pint in your tote bag."

"I walked all the way from Victoria bloody station." Margaret blew her nose long and hard in her huge hanky. Peggy winced.

"Goodbye then," said Margaret. "You'll be all right then?"

"Yes."

"You won't watch those horrid home movies?"

"No."

"Liar. Every time we turned around you were bringing out those horrid old cassettes you made of Willy. They bored us shitless. They bored Willy too! Shitless."

"Like you and your fake diarrhea?! Shitless? Willy told me about you and your fake diarrhea. It was a lark for Willy. You were a pushover. He did not respect you."

"Liar! Your home movies are sick! Your lying, little cassettes are sick! Sick!"

"Go, Margaret! For chrissake, go!"

"Go?! Where?! Where shall I go?!"

"Go to Hell!" cried Peggy.

"I am in Hell!" shrieked Margaret and sank miserably back on the stone ledge, blew her nose yet again then stood, dabbing at her eyes with a flowered silk scarf. "Cow!" She shouted, and adjusted her matching flowered skirt which had been tugged round back to front. "You'll be all right then?"

"I will be all right," said Peggy.

"Yes!" called Margaret, making her wobbly way up the three stone steps to the street from where she turned and shouted "Sure! You'll be all right! But what about bloody me?! It's dark! I'll be attacked by rapists. I'll be a statistic tomorrow! You're a cow!" she shouted as she clacked, sobbing, on her inappropriate heels, down the dimly lit, cobbled street.

Peggy crouched deep into Willy's reading chair, listening as Margaret's footsteps grew faint. Safe at last from Margaret's prying eyes, she jumped up, switched on a light and rushed to the hall wardrobe where she whipped out Willy's huge, green satin dressing gown and pulled it on over her slip and tied it at her waist. Perhaps not as fussily as Willy might have tied it, with a perfectly formed bow, but carefully and lovingly. From Willy's desk drawer she again took his revolver and placed it on the desk. From the bottom of the wardrobe she lifted out a small film projector, set it out and removed a painting from the wall and aimed the projector at the cleared space. Taking a reel of film from a box in the wardrobe, she threaded it into the projector, switched it on and sat, opened her eyes wide.

An exceptionally handsome young man in a swimsuit sat on the tiny lawn of a small, enclosed garden, their back garden. He looked up, noted the camera on him, rose and grinned. The film frames began to catch and rattle and the film broke and flapped and the projection's rectangle on the wall went blank. Peggy couldn't move, sat transfixed as the film reel continued to rattle and flap.

Early next morning, still in Willy's dressing gown, Peggy was at Willy's desk, a tray of tea and toast beside her. The projector and the revolver were in place but the reel of damaged film was in her lap and between sips of tea she attempted to repair the broken piece of film with tape. The telephone rang. She swallowed a bit of toast with a gulp of tea, answered. "Hello."

"You said you were going to Yorkshire."

"Top of the morning to ye, Margaret."

"You're not in Yorkshire," said very sullen Margaret.

"No. I'm apparently here, keepin' the home fires burnin'. Top of the morning to ye."

"You said you were going to Yorkshire. Liar."

"I didn't go to Yorkshire. As I explained, I am here. Beside my petit déjeuner. Or, breakfast, to the great unwashed which surely includes you. Have you bothered to wash yourself this week?"

"Are you all right?" said Margaret.

"Are you?"

"No. Can I come over?"

"No."

"You are a wicked woman, Peggy."

"I'm much too nice, Maggie."

"What are you doing?"

"Drinking breakfast tea."

"You were dreadful, yesterday. Sending me home in the dark. I could have been raped."

"And were you?" asked Peggy as she fumbled with a crumbling bit of film.

"No."

"Jolly good."

"You were dreadful."

"Funerals are dreadful. What do you want?"

"Something of Willy's," moaned Margaret, "A book?"

Peggy buttered a piece of toast, took a bite, washed it down with tea, said "Can you read?"

"Don't be spiteful, Peggy."

"Sure I'll give you a book, Mar-gar-et."

"Oh. So you're mar-gar-reting me again?"

"What book do you want?"

Margaret sniffled, sneezed and blew her nose. Peggy held the telephone away from her ear.

"Any book. So long as it was Willy's," snuffled Margaret. "Peggy, I've been crying for two days."

Peggy took another bit of toast, another sip of tea. "He's got a lovely book on Genital Herpes," said Peggy, munching toast as she spoke. "Lavishly illustrated. How would you like a book about Genital Herpes? Lavishly illustrated."

Peggy waited.

"When are you going to Yorkshire?" said Margaret.

"Soon."

"What is it, Peggy?!"

"My fucking husband died! He wasn't supposed to! I am forty-two fucking years old and my fucking husband's kicked the fucking bucket!"

"I am coming over!" cried Margaret.

"I won't let you in!"

"Then I'm calling a doctor!"

"Why? Are you ill?"

"No. You are!"

"Yeah! I'm bloody sick of you!"

Peggy took another bite of toast and a swallow of tea. Margaret took a swallow of whisky, whispered sweetly into her telephone, "Will you ring me when you come back from Yorkshire?"

"How much did you love Willy?" asked Peggy, calmly attempting to join two bits of film.

"I loved you both. Equally."

"Answer, please."

"It was a very long time ago, Peggy."

"Was he just a good screw or what?"

"It was a very long time ago."

"I think he was. A good screw. An excellent screw. An incomparable screw. N'est-ce-pas?"

"Yes." said Margaret, "To all the above. Times ten."

"Darling, Willy fucked anything of either sex that was warm, cute or just couldn't get away."

Margaret was silent as she shook her head, set down the telephone and her glass and blew her nose.

"He never told you he loved you?" said Peggy.

"No."

"Did you tell him you loved him?"

Margaret was silent.

"Did you tell him you loved him?!" screamed Peggy.

"YES-YES-YES-YES-YES!" cried Margaret. Peggy, we've been through all of --"

"What did he say?" commanded Peggy.

"Peggy, please!"

"What did the sneaky bastard say?!"

"Don't you dare speak to me like --"

"I'll tell you what that sneaky American bastard said! He said tough shit, baby! That's what he said! He said tough shit, baby! I love my wife, Peggeen!"

"Those were his exact words," whispered Margaret, defeated.

"You have an awful effect on people, Mar-gar-et."

"Maggie is my name."

"Do you still want a book, Mar-gar-et? It's lavishly illustrated."

"Ring me, please," slurred Margaret. "When you come back from..."

"I said: Do you still want a book? Willy's got another

book about particularly nasty sexually transmitted diseases. Wonderfully detailed photos! In glorious colour! You, of all people, would love it, kid! It would be a stroll down memory lane."

"It was Trichomoniasis! It is very common!" cried Margaret.

"Like you, duckie?"

"Please ring me when --"

"Sure!"

Peggy slammed down the telephone, took a hefty swallow of tea. The telephone rang. She set down her cup and lifted the receiver but before she could speak Margaret screamed "COW!" and rang off. Peggy laughed, choked on her tea. She saw Willy's pipe on the floor, picked it up and studied it for a moment, licking the stem, tasting. She frowned, put it back in its rack with the others. On her knees she gathered up several bits of broken film that had flapped away the night before and dropped them and the film reel in a paper bag. She found a local business directory in a desk drawer, thumbed through it, found a page and wrote down an address, slipped it in her handbag and disappeared up the stairs to change.

Tim, a youngish, red-haired salesclerk, watched Peggy with interest as she moved about peering anxiously at various video/television displays in the shop. She wasn't a knockout -- not by a long shot -- definitely an older woman. But older women were attractive and she looked sad and Tim was a nice, sympathetic, youngish man. Peggy had just become aware of Tim and occasionally glanced at him in a perfectly friendly, innocent way. He approached and lingered near as she earnestly watched a love-scene on a display television. Not turning away from the love-scene, she spoke. "I have a little problem."

"Yeah?"

"Yeah. I have a very old movie. My own," said Peggy casually. "I made it my own clever self..."

Peggy hesitated, losing her confidence instantly. What if he thought she was flirting with him?

"Yeah?" replied Tim, somewhat more attractive than when she'd first noticed him. Was it the love-scene on the video-television display that so affected her?

"Yeah," she said, turned and smiled uncertainly.

"So?" he said.

"So. It's falling to bits..."

"Yeah?" said Tim. He grinned. Not so engagingly as Willy might have grinned, but...

"Yeah..." she said, hesitated.

"And?" Tim grinned again. This time it was easily as nice a grin as Willy ever produced -- even on special occasions.

"My film...it's of great sentimental value. I don't want to lose it. It crumbles, literally crumbles away in my fingers when I try to put it into the projector. It's such an old projector." Peggy launched a tiny, crisp laugh. "I wonder if... "

"Yeah?"

"Do you make, I mean, do you do...conversions? Can you errr convert me?" She laughed again, her crisp little laugh. How was he to know she could hardly place one word after another? "Can you make," said Peggy, "Can you make a what-do-they-call-them? A video..."

"Videocassette?" said Tim.

"Can you make a videocassette thingy from my crumbly old film? It's a silent film -- I mean it's quite simple, homemade, no sound. Silent. Old. And as I said, crumbly. Do you do that sort of thing?"

Am I flirting? thought Peggy. What do they call it these days? I'm so...out of touch. Yes, I'm flirting. He knows it. Is he flirting too?

"Yeah. We do that sort of thing," said Tim, grinning again, a grin that dwarfed Willy's grin. It was the Academy Award of grins.

Peggy turned, touched the display videocassette player.

"I suppose I'll need one of these, won't I? To play the video thingy on?"

"Yeah."

"Are they complicated? I'm hopeless." She wasn't at all hopeless, but technically very competent and she knew it -- *what on earth am I playing at? I'm making a fool of myself.*

"Yeah. You'll need one."

"Then I'd better buy one, hadn't I? A videocassette player."

"What kind?"

"The kind that plays videocassettes, I suppose." Peggy laughed. "Is there any other kind?" She laughed again. *Jesus! Either he has absolutely no sense of humour or I'm being a complete idiot.*

Peggy unconsciously caressed the video playing the love-scene, said "This kind. Do you deliver?"

"Yeah," said Tim.

"Are they difficult to manoeuvre?"

"I can show you how."

"Can you show me how when you deliver?" Peggy felt she was now definitely in the swing of it. It wasn't so difficult talking to strangers, flirting -- if that's what they did call it these days -- flirting with strangers. Attractive, youngish strangers.

"I'm on the technical side, myself," said Tim.

"Really?!" said Peggy louder than she'd intended.

"I don't normally deliver," he said.

He doesn't care at all! Jesus! Just what am I after? I am a fool! But she heard herself saying, "I'm nearby. That little Georgian street just off Vincent Square. Maunsel Street. It's only a few minutes walk from here."

Peggy glanced anxiously out the display window, held her breath. It was already dark. She'd sent Margaret, alone, into this same, scary abyss last night.

"That's real near," said Tim and grinned again. *It's all right,* thought Peggy, and breathed out. She could continue...

flirting? What a funny word. What an innocent word. She was an innocent too. Before she'd met Willy who was not.

"Real near," continued Peggy in what she'd thought was, but wasn't, Tim's own lingo, the youngish man. Tim, whose eye she had definitely caught. "That's why your ad attracted me. You're so... convenient. I'd be happy to pay you extra for your time. You could do it on your own time. I'd be very grateful."

"Yeah?" said Tim, grinning.

"Yeah," said Peggy, "I'm...desperate." An admission she had not meant to make. But she felt her face was a blank. Or at least a parody of desperation that couldn't possibly be taken seriously by anyone. But was. By him, and he said -- with a seriousness that must always, Peggy now knew, must always be taken very seriously -- "I can do it." And Peggy said "Oh, can you?" She meant every word.

"Yeah. Sure I can."

"And my film conversion? My video-what's-it?"

"Videocassette, love"

Now she had been addressed as 'love'! And she said "How soon can you...convert me?" and launched again her crisp, little laugh. "It's important. I'll pay for the extra service."

"I'll do it all myself," he said, grinning again. He seemed to Peggy, the very happiest of volunteers and she grinned back and said "How soon?"

"Tomorrow," said Tim. "Look, we're closing in a few minutes so if you can drop the film in our night slot I can --"

Peggy thrust her paper bag into his hands, pleadingly regarded him.

"I'll have everything in your hands by tomorrow night," promised Tim.

"Everything? In my hands?"

"Yeah. Everything. Tomorrow."

"You will be careful with the film? It's fragile."

"I'm always real careful. 'Specially if it's fragile," he grinned, yet again lighting up the shop.

"You are an angel. Everything, then. Tomorrow, Angel."

Tim took a pencil from behind his ear and a note pad from his shirt pocket. "Name?"

Peggy gazed wonderingly at him. Taller than Willy. Eyes, blue-green. Hair, red and curly. Skin, pink and somewhat freckled.

"Name?" he repeated.

"Peggeen."

Tim grinned and, pencil in hand, brushed a large red curl from his eye, waited for the rest of her information.

Peggy left the video shop, shivered and pulled her coat tighter, paused and turned to catch a last look at Tim who was now speaking to another customer. She began to walk quickly toward Vincent Square for the short but lonely walk home. It would be her first evening walk without Willy. Damn him.

Peggy, small in the vast, dark expanse of the square, paused by the playing field. Suddenly here was Willy in his rugby shorts, running hard. She knew she had seen only the dancing lights across the grass but... A cat howled, she jumped and began to hurry, a dog barked, she hurried faster, heard a rustle in some bushes, began to run.

Peggy was terrified. Running down deserted, cobbled Maunsel Street, she knew that someone was running not far behind her. At her house she fumbled with the key, dropped it. The running footsteps approached alarmingly. On her knees, panicking, she found her key, opened the door, threw herself in and slammed and bolted it shut. Wide-eyed and panting, she hovered at the door, peering out through its tiny window.

A young man carrying a bouquet of flowers rushed by. Peggy was breathless, gaped at him as he presented the flowers to a happy young woman in the house opposite.

Peggy screamed as the telephone rang. She ran to Willy's desk, lifted the receiver, did not speak.

"Peggy?! Peggy?!"

Peggy could not speak, could only pant into the telephone.

"Peggy, what is it?" cried Margaret.

"They're chasing me!" cried Peggy.

"Who is chasing you?!"

"Men with flowers!"

"What?!"

"No one."

"No one?!" said Margaret.

"I'm a liar," said Peggy.

"You're breathless!" cried Margaret, "Why are you breathless?!"

"I'm exercising," said Peggy. "You should too, Mags. Your arse is flat. I need a bath. G'bye!"

"Stay away from Willy's razors!" cried Margaret.

Peggy slammed down the telephone, struggled out of her coat and threw it on a chair. She found Willy's dressing gown on the floor by his desk and slipped it on. She went to the kitchen, set on the kettle, grabbed two cups from the cupboard, frowned, put one back and set the other on the tea tray. She stared at the single cup for a moment, reconsidered, put it back in the cupboard and switched off the gas and set the kettle back on the sideboard. She returned to Willy's desk, sighed, took a small box of cassettes and an audiocassette player from its drawer, inserted a cassette and sat waiting. The cassette began:

> "You're joking, Peggy!"
> "I'm not."
> "You are!"
> "Why won't you?"
> "It's too silly, Peg! But if you'll turn that damned thing off, I will!"
> "No, Willy! Just say it, for chrissake, just say I love you!"

"I love you. There!"
"Say I love *you*, Peggeen."
"I love *you*, Peggeen."
"Not so difficult. Was it?" (both laugh)

Peggy pressed the fast-forward switch for a moment, released it:

"Say it! Say it! Go on! Say exactly
what you said to her! (sobbing) Go on!
Exactly what you said to her!"
"Tough shit, baby!
I love Peggeen!"

Peggy the widow glowered at the cassette player, whispered "You sonofabitch!"

"I love *you*, Peggeen!"
"(sobbing) Say it again, you sonofabitch!"
"I love *you*, Peggeen."

Peggy clicked off the cassette player. "You sonofabitch!" she said and leapt from Willy's desk chair and switched off the lights and ran up the stairs to the bedroom -- hers and Willy's bedroom.

It was late afternoon the following day that the doorbell rang. It was Tim in his Sunday best, a large box in his arms. He rang again. After what seemed several minutes to him, but wasn't, Peggy, in a stylish, low-cut dress and newly made-up, a drink in her hand, hurried down the stairs to greet him.

"Angel!" she said, pulling him happily through the door, "I thought you'd never come!"

Peggy, only a bit merry, motioned where to put the box and his handsome, youngish self. She offered him a scotch from Willy's chic little bar which he gladly accepted as he unwrapped the videocassette player. From the box he also took the old film reel and the new videocassette and handed them to Peggy. She cast the old film at a chair and clutched the videocassette to her breast and cried "Thank you, Angel!"

"Nice place you got here, Missus," said Tim.

"It was Willy's. Is Willy's," she said, but quickly added "And mine too. Mine too! Of course!" and tried to laugh. Perhaps she'd had more than one scotch -- she wasn't counting. It was hard to know, particularly at a time like this with everything in flux. She wasn't a drinker at all. Perhaps that was the trouble.

"Nice." Tim looked about. "Yeah. It sure is. Your place. Real nice."

"Yeah," said Peggy, "yeah, it sure is. Bottoms up!" Peggy drank. It was a larger swallow than anticipated and she choked as he grinned sympathetically. He was a good man. A gentle man. She was certain of it. He had to be.

"Nice. Yeah," said Tim, raising his glass and quaffing. "Where's the telly then?"

"This is Willy's study. He's a doctor," said Peggy. "A brain surgeon."

"Nice. Real nice," said Tim. "Where's the telly then?"

"What telly?" asked Peggy, pouring another for Tim and one for herself just to be sociable.

"You got to have a telly, Missus, to play your video on. The videocassette plays through the telly like. You got to have a telly."

"A telly?!" said Peggy, splashing her scotch.

"Yeah," said Tim, draining his own glass which Peggy moved in quickly to fill, saying, "We -- I -- we don't have a telly."

"No telly?" said Tim, believing this impossible, particularly for an attractive, well-off woman certainly not *that* much older than him. "You ain't got no telly then?"

Peggy went to the newly unwrapped videocassette player, thumped it ferociously.

"Doesn't this contraption, have its own err...screen-thingy? I thought they all had their own screen-thingies somewhere."

"No. They ain't."

"Why didn't you tell me that before?!" cried Peggy.

"Everybody's got a telly, Missus."

"I -- we --I don't!" said Peggy,

"Look, Missus. I'm sorry you got no telly. It ain't my fault you got no telly."

"Must you call me Missus?!" cried Peggy.

"Look, lady, I'm sorry."

"Can you get one?"

"Now? It's gone six."

"Can you get a television for me now?"

"Now?!"

"ARE YOU DEAF?! *NOW*!"

"Hey-hey-hey!" said Tim, backing away. What was her problem, what she was about? His girlfriend, Angela, had a problem too. His boss. But maybe that was his problem, not hers.

"God! I'm sorry!" said Peggy with a look so forlorn Tim would have walked to the end of the world for her -- he would do it in a minute! He was a good man.

"I am really awfully sorry," moaned Peggy.

"You want a telly?"

Peggy nodded pathetically.

"What kind do you want?"

"Jesus, I don't know! One that plays videocassettes?"

"Let's put it this way," said Tim as patiently, as gently as he could -- he was kind man too. "Let's put it this way. How much do you want to pay?"

"I don't bloody care," said Peggy, pouring another drink for each of them. "How much will you need?"

They worked it out and Peggy lead Tim to Willy's desk,

took out a small metal box and from it counted notes into his hand until he said "Hey! That's enough."

It was more than enough and Tim knew it. But you never really knew, like. Anyhow, she would have the difference back. He'd see to that. He was an honest man. His mother had said so many times. "Be back as soon as I can," he said. "Be an hour." He was out the door but poked his head back in, said, "Are you all right... Peggeen?"

"Everybody keeps asking me if I'm all right. Of course I'm not all right. I only need a television."

He was gone. Peggy sat, poured another scotch. Was miserable -- felt stupid and out of control. She had been stupid and she was out of control. At least tonight. Why not? She was a widow and he had called her Peggeen. Be back as soon as I can, he'd said, and are you all right... Peggeen?

Peggy splashed more ice-cubes into her glass at Willy's chic little bar. Willy had been the drinker, not her. But now, she would try it on for herself. So far, it fit. She smiled when she heard Tim's car start up and drive away. Glass in hand, she returned to Willy's desk, sat and stared at nothing and stirred her drink with her finger and thought of Tim and Willy. Would they have liked one another? Probably. Damn you, Willy! She yanked open the desk drawer, saw Willy's revolver and a few scattered bullets. The telephone rang. She slammed the drawer shut and glared at the telephone, allowed it to ring several times before she lifted the receiver, said, "Yeah?!"

"Jean, dear."

"Hello, Jean-dear."

"Mags said you hadn't left yet. Left for Yorkshire."

"I've left, Jean-dear. I just haven't arrived."

"What?"

Peggy took a long, purposely noisy swallow.

"Well. Maggie says you're having a bit of a rough time. You wouldn't let her in yesterday or something. She was forced to walk home on heels in the dark."

"She should have walked on her toes. A heel will let you down every time. Take it from me."

Jean seemed not to have heard and said "Something silly like that. You know Maggie's overactive imagination."

"Jean-dear?"

"Yes, Peggy?"

"I can't remember. Do you and Jack have a telly?"

"We have three. Two of them were the children's, of course, before they moved out. Black and whites. Ancient."

"We, I mean I, don't even have one. Isn't that funny?" said Peggy. "I never thought of it before tonight. Isn't it peculiar not having a telly? Isn't it odd? Isn't it...perverted? We were perverts, Jean. I am convinced that Willy and I were perverts."

"Don't be silly. Willy never watched television, did he? He was opposed to television -- made a great show of it. That doesn't make one a pervert. Willy simply never watched television."

"No. I suppose that's why we never got one."

"Well, yes," said Jean.

"Willy preferred carousing to telly-viewing," said Peggy taking another swallow from Willy's favourite, cut-crystal whisky glass. "Jean-dear?"

"Yes, love?"

"Why didn't we have a telly for me, Jean-dear? I might have wanted to watch something. Films, drama. Even the news. The awful news. John Lennon's been shot you know."

"I heard. Isn't it awful?" said Jean.

"Everybody seems to be dying these days. In one way or another. It's a fad, isn't it? Wouldn't you call it a fad, Jean-dear?"

"Well. I wouldn't go so far as to say that." Jean frowned into her telephone -- this was most peculiar. "But, well, about the telly. Why didn't you just go out and buy one? You were the one with the legacy."

"It never occurred to me. If Willy didn't want a telly it never occurred to me that I might."

"Well. There you are, dear. That's it in a nutshell, isn't it?"

"Yes. In a nutshell." Peggy took another swallow. Jean heard the glass clink and hoped that Peggy had not gone astray like their unfortunate Margaret.

"We did have our...playthings, Willy and I. Our tape recorders, our film cameras..."

"Of course you did, dear. Your life was..." Jean paused.

"Was what?"

"Well. Filled. Full. Wasn't it?"

"Full of Willy," said Peggy. "Bursting with Willy."

Jean was silent.

"Jean-dear?"

"Yes, love?"

"Did you and Jack say Willy and Peggy or Peggy and Willy"?

"How do you mean?"

"When you referred to us. Did you say Willy and Peggy or Peggy and Willy?"

"Well. Let's see. Well. I believe we said both."

Peggy, held up her empty glass, stared through its bottom at the old framed photo of her preternaturally handsome Willy.

"Then, I take it you mean that sometimes you said Willy and Peggy and sometimes you said Peggy and Willy? Or did you always say both each time one right after the other?"

"I really don't see what difference it makes, love."

"I wondered what you said, that's all. When you referred to us." Peggy poured another. Jean heard, frowned again into her telephone.

"Assuming," said Peggy, "that you referred to us at all."

Jean was becoming jumpy with this odd, pointless conversation and was determined to end it as soon as she could. After all, she had only wanted to help. "When are you going to Yorkshire?" she asked. "We could have lunch and I could drive you to the train. You are going by train?"

"Oh God, yes! By train! I've not even packed yet. So much to do. So little time. I certainly would drive myself to the station if I'd learned to drive."

"Ah. Well," said Jean. "But then you'd have a parking problem, wouldn't you? Where on earth could you park the car? You'd have to walk miles. And with a suitcase!"

"An overnight case," corrected Peggy. "Why didn't I learn to drive?"

"Honestly, dear. You are a big silly. Willy drove, didn't he? How long will you be gone?"

"Gone?"

"Yorkshire, dear. How long will you be gone?"

"Long as it takes."

"How d'you mean?"

"Willy's aunt. She's gone off the deep end. She wasn't a rock in the best of times and she's ancient now. Willy was her favourite."

"Willy was everybody's favourite," offered Jean.

"Wasn't he just?! Everybody's favourite! Do you know how old she is? She is ninety-nine. The ugly old hag is ninety-nine!"

"What? What did you say, dear?!"

"Ninety-nine if she's a day! At least she looks ninety-nine, feels ninety-nine. Though I've never asked. It's just an assumption. Ain't it, Jeanie-dear? We must presume to presume, mustn't we? We are labouring, as it were, under the most extenuating circumstances."

Peggy took another swallow from her glass, clinked it loudly against her teeth so Jean would hear. Jean heard, knew, frowned yet again into her telephone, worried for a millisecond, said "Well, oh my. I've never really thought --"

"How right you are, love -- poor old thing's jumped off the deep end, has Auntie. Can you hold on a sec, Jean-dear? I was about to pour myself a little nippie when you rang. Calms the spirits -- pardon my pun. Can you hold on?"

"Of course," said Jean, checking the time on her exquisite

Cartier wristwatch.

Peggy swallowed the last of the bottle beside her, went to Willy's bar, poured another, returned, flopped into Willy's desk chair, and took up the telephone. "Poor old Auntie. Rings me constantly. Sobs her old heart out. I have to shriek my condolences into the telephone because the darling old thing is stone deaf."

"Poor darling old thing," sighed Jean.

"But she never asks me how I feel. She should be offering me condolences. She never inquires about my sudden and most unexpected loss. I mean, Jeanie-dear, how often does ones beloved hubby just up and kick the proverbial bucket at the ripe old age of forty-nine? Don't you dare say only once!" Peggy melted into uproarious laughter, choked on a swallow of scotch.

"You must calm yourself, love," said Jean. "You've had a terrible shock."

"Poor, poor Auntie," said Peggy, suddenly quieting down.

"Poor darling old thing," agreed Jean.

"Of course we must make allowances for the excessively old and spectacularly self-centered. She's ninety-nine, you know. We do turn inward with age and one must be understanding. Yes. Willy was her favourite. But then, Jean, as you so succinctly put it, Willy was everybody's favourite."

"Yes, he was. Indeed he was," sighed Jean.

"Yes, indeedy-do!" chirped Peggy, "Was Willy your favourite, Jeanie-weenie?"

"We all loved Willy, didn't we, dear?"

"Didn't we ever! How much did you love Willy, Jeanie-weenie?"

Jean stiffened, said "Well. No more and no less than I should have."

"How much was that then, lovey?"

"Jack and I are going to be over your way in a bit. Smith Square. Chamber music. Pergolesi, I believe. Or was it

Cimarosa? Will you come with us? We've got three tickets."

"No."

"Do you mind if we stop by after the concert for a minute?" said Jean quickly, "only a minute?"

"Why? Do you want one of his books too? Margaret's begging for a book. Well, Jean...well..." said Peggy the mimic, "...well. You can't have one. I've given them all away -- to a home for wayward girls. Kept all my own books and given all of Willy's away. He'd have wanted that. He adored wayward girls. And now I have a place, at last, for all my own fucking books! Isn't that fortuitous?"

"Err...in a manner of speaking." Jean checked her Cartier again. "Honestly, Peggy, We'd only stay for a minute. Promise. One minute. Jack's worried about you."

"Only Jack? Aren't you worried too, Jeanie?"

"Of course I am... dear. That goes without saying."

"But Jack's being worried doesn't go without saying? Jack's being worried is a fucking event?!"

"Please! We both love you very much, Peggy, darling. We love you very, very much. We promise to stay for only one minute."

"Only one minute?" cried Peggy. "That's love?!"

"Darling. Don't be a big silly. You know very well what --"

"So sorry. Your presence would not be convenient. I have an engagement."

"Engagement?"

"A young merchant is calling on me this evening."

"Young merchant?!"

"Jesus Chee-rist! Has the whole fucking world gone stone deaf?!"

"Peggy! That was uncalled for!"

"I am receiving a visit from a young man who sells things."

"Oh. What sort of things?" asked Jean matter-of-factly.

"Televisions. Videos. Birth control pills. Wristwatches -- some lovely Cartier fakes. Have you verified yours lately,

Jeanie? The young man says there are scads of fake Cartiers about, simply scads!"

"He said that, did he?" said Jean, squinting carefully at her Cartier.

"Look, Jean-dear. I've got to pee."

"Oh Peggy, don't be crude."

"Crude? Who's crude?" said Peggy. "It's just my goddamned bladder. The one fucking thing I can still count on to inconvenience me!"

"Peggy, darling! You can count on your friends!"

"And who might they be? These alleged friends?"

"You can count on Jack and me and Maggie, that's who!"

"Two posh snobs and a drunk! Why don't I feel comforted?"

"Don't be a big silly. Will you promise to ring me tomorrow? If you don't promise to ring me tomorrow, Jack and I will drop by tonight and that's a promise. Do you promise?"

"I will ring you tomorrow."

"Promise?"

"I pwomise," lisped Peggy, the naughty child.

"Well. Goodnight, Peggy."

"Nighty-night, Jeanie-weenie!" lisped Peggy and slammed down the telephone.

Peggy sashayed into the small loo under the staircase, hitched up her dress and sat herself serenely on the toilet. She cackled, immediately rose and went to Willy's desk, switched on the cassette player, returned and sat again, listening with glee as she peed.

> "If you laugh, Peg, I'll stop.
> That's a promise.
> Do you promise not to
> laugh?" (Peggy giggles)
> "Stop that, Peg! Do you
> promise? No laughing?"
> "I pwomise, Willy!"

"All right, here goes...
Yellow-blue sky
Yellow-blue beach
People reclining
Just out of my reach
With my hand in the sand
I burrow for pleasure
But stealthily..."
"You should have said *and*, Willy, it's
more sonorous. *And* stealthily."
"*And* stealthily, not to impinge
on their leisure
I catch a quick look
and go back to my book."

"You selfish sonofabitch!" cried the squatting widow from her toilet seat, "You wouldn't buy me a telly!"

"You're very gifted, Willy!"

"Like hell he is!" screamed widow-Peggy.

"I love you, Willy, darling!"
"Me too, Peggeen. I love you too!"

Peggy, squatting there, made a terrible face. She grabbed her glass from the wash-basin, quaffed it, grabbed a tissue, patted herself dry -- always pat, never, *never* rub, Mother had warned -- flushed the toilet and rushed to Willy's desk. She pressed the fast-forward on the player and the voices squealed crazily for a moment then:

"You're squashing me, Willy! (Grunt)
Let me up!"
"No, darling, I have a proposition."

"Get off! You're squashing me!"
"Better?"
"Better."
"I have a proposition, Peg."
"Steady on, mate. We're being recorded
for posterity."
"That's the question, Peggy, darling.
Posterity. Shall we have one?"
"One what?"
"A posterity. A baby, darling."
"Turn off this damned machine! Willy!
Turn off this goddamned machine!"
(Click)

"I am a cow..." whispered Peggy, dozing off in Willy's leather desk chair. "I am a sodding cow."

She slept. Sometime later the telephone rang startling her awake.

"Hello!" snapped Peggy.

"I'm sorry," said Margaret.

"For what?" snapped Peggy, her eyes blinking with sleep.

"You're not a cow."

"Oh, but I am, Margaret!"

Margaret was near tears. "You're not!" she cried. "You are absolutely not!"

"I am," said Peggy, "I could have had a calf. I'm a cow. Cows have calves. I didn't have a calf but I'm still a cow."

"No! Peggy! You're not!" sniffled Margaret.

Peggy knew that at this moment Margaret was wiping her eyes. Peggy knew that Margaret was also having a snort of whisky. Snort was such a Willy word. Peggy smiled. Her anger eased. But only a moment.

"No, you're not," insisted Margaret, in full sob. "Not a cow. What are you doing?"

"Sleeping. What time is it?"

"Around ten. Yes. Ten P.M. Nighttime."

"I've been robbed," said Peggy.

"Robbed?! My God!" cried Margaret, upsetting her glass. "How much?!"

"Seven hundred quid."

"My God! Have you called the police?! Did they hurt you?! Were you assaulted?! Who was it?! My God! I'm coming over!"

"You'd miss the last tube back."

"I can afford a taxi."

"No you can't," said Peggy.

"No. I can't. Did they wear a mask?"

"Who?"

"You're lying, aren't you?" hissed Margaret.

"No."

"Who was it then? Who robbed you?!"

"Nobody. Me."

"Peggy. Please!"

"I robbed me. I robbed Willy."

"Peggy!"

"I'm dry. Need a refill. S'cuse me whilst I refill my cup, which don't at the moment, exactly runneth over."

"Darling? You shouldn't drink alone. I should be there with you. We could reminisce. Peggy, darling? Peggy?! Are you there?"

Peggy returned with another scotch, took a swallow and picked up the telephone, said, "I could have had a child."

"No you couldn't."

"Could. Didn't."

"Who took your seven hundred pounds?!"

"Seven hundred *quid*," corrected Peggy.

"What do you mean you could have had a child?"

"I was physically able to gestate a huu-man child."

"I don't believe you. Willy wanted a child more than anything in the world. Willy was so beautiful. It would have been an angel. That child would have been an angel."

"I was Willy's angel!"

"God only knows why you didn't have a child. According to Willy, you were rabbits!"

"We screwed whole days away," mused Peggy. "We barely stopped for air. Shut ourselves in a room, any room. On a table or a chair or the floor. We screwed and screwed and screwed."

"So you would say and say and say," hissed Margaret.

"Shut up. I was on the pill," said Peggy, "Willy didn't know I was on the pill."

"Liar! How could he not?! Willy was a doctor! That beautiful man was a doctor! He had to know!"

"He was a brain surgeon, darling," said Peggy, with only a tinge of a slur. "Brain surgeons deal with absolutely nothing below the waist. It's a thing with them. Some haughty…thing. Makes 'em feel superior. He probably thought I was a freak or something. A freak with a super-secret, mysteriously impene- trable inner membrane that shunned his too-eager sperma- tozoa."

Peggy laughed and slurped a swallow. "He never really understood me. I faked my fertility tests too -- at that quack's in Harley street who'd have done anything for a kind word from famous Dr Willy's wife. And I lied to Willy. Lied and lied and lied!"

"Liar!"

"C'est moi!"

"Peggy, have you been drinking?"

"Of course, I've been drinking! I'm in mourning, for God's sake! And -- need I ask -- have you?"

"Oh, Peggy! I'll come over!"

"Why? Out of booze? No. You can't come over. You'd miss the last tube back."

"I could stay over," pleaded Margaret.

"No. I'm expecting a young merchant."

"A young what?"

"I hired me a hooker," laughed Peggy.

"You've been drinking."

"So I said."

"Go to bed, Peggy, it's late. When do you leave for Yorkshire?"

"When I'm damn good and ready. Tomorrow."

"I'll see you off."

"No. I'm being driven. Why should I consort with you? I've finished consorting with you. You slept with Willy."

"Who's driving you to the train?"

"My hooker."

"You don't hire hookers!"

"Sez who?!"

"You're drunk!" cried Margaret.

"So are you. Willy always said you were a lush. That's why Willy chose me. 'Cause you're a goddamned lush, Mar-gar-ret.

"Liar!"

"Even though you were prettier, Willy chose me because you are a goddamned lushy-lush-lush! Whilst I...I, a librarian, am dependable!"

"Dependable? All you ever had was a legacy! You liar!"

"Refute at your peril. I have it all in black in white. On a tape. I'll play it for you sometime. I cannot abide loopy lushes, blotto bitches, daffy drunks, says my Willy to me. Margaret's a lush and I therefore cannot abide her."

"Liar!"

"You're not even pretty anymore, Mar-gar-et. Lushes lose looks early!"

"Liar! You put Willy up to that! With your damned tape recorder! He hated that tape recorder! He told me so! Lies! Silly, juvenile lies! You drove him mad! You told Willy what to say on your infernal machine and you told him lies! And now, it seems, now it seems, you even lied about your fucking uterus!"

"It was my fucking uterus! Mine!" screamed Peggy.

"Well you haven't got it anymore, have you?! I held your

hand when they scooped it out! It's gone! And a fat lot of good a uterus did you, you lying bitch!"

"Hey! I'm in mourning. Remember?"

Peggy stirred her ice-cubes, gently amused.

"I'd better hang up," whispered Margaret, "before I say something dreadful."

Peggy threw herself back in Willy's chair and laughed.

"What's so damned funny?!"

"You are, pet."

"What did I say, Peggy, that was so...laughable?"

"Nothing, Mags, nothing."

"We've been drinking, haven't we, Peggy?"

"Yes, pet."

"I miss him so," whimpered Margaret.

"Me too."

"Me too," whimpered Margaret.

"Go to bed," said Peggy, softly.

"I should be with you, Peggy. Because we love each other. We're all we've got now, aren't we?"

"We've got Jean and Jack. They threatened to call this evening."

"Pooh on Jean and Jack," said Margaret.

"Have you noticed how we always say Jean first? Jean and Jack? Doesn't say much for poor Jack, does it?"

"Pooh on Jean and Jack."

"Goodnight, Maggie."

"Look," said Margaret, "I could get dressed and stagger out to a cab and..."

"No. I wouldn't let you in. Goodnight, Maggie."

"Goodnight, Peggy," whispered Margaret and began to blow her nose.

Peggy sighed, put down the telephone, drained her glass and sighed again. The doorbell rang and she brightened, checked her makeup, smiled for effect, arranged her low-cut dress and opened the door. It was Tim with a large carton.

Peggy grinned wildly as she showed him in -- she was not a seasoned drinker, couldn't help that it showed. "Angel!" she cried, "I thought you'd flown!"

"Sorry. Had to go way out to --"

"Never mind, love. Care for a drink? Mind if I do?"

Tim set the carton on a table.

"Had to get it from the warehouse. Didn't cost near so much as I reckoned so you got a whole lot coming back." He offered her a wad of notes.

"Keep it, love," said Peggy, pouring drinks at Willy's little bar, "for services rendered above and beyond the call of duty."

Tim gladly pocketed the money. He was a good man but he was a working man too and a little extra, well, a lot of extra... "Yeah," he said, thanks. I'm not so much on the selling side of the telly business, you see. I'm a technician. A trouble-shooter, you know? I was only filling in yesterday at the shop."

"Yeah, said Peggy, handing his drink, "put the TV there, love, by the video-whatsis."

Tim politely set down his glass and unpacked the television and, on his knees, connected it to the video as Peggy, watched and lightly flirted -- is that what they called it these days? She kneeled so close behind him that when he turned he found his nose was nearly resting between her breasts.

"Hey! You're dangerous!" laughed Peggy. "Au secours, constable! Au secours!" She handed him his glass.

"Tah," said Tim and drank, and motioned at the video. "She's ready to go."

"Oh," said Peggy, laughing again, "you mean the video!"

Tim grinned and switched on the television, sat down, sat back and said "Whaddaya think?"

"Lovely! That's what I think!"

Peggy nestled, nearly disappearing, into Willy's huge reading chair. "Now I can watch from Willy's favourite chair."

"Your husband out, is he?"

"Yeah."

"Cassette, please," said Tim.

"Roger! Let's get this show on the road," said Peggy who hugged the videocassette to her breast, kissed it and handed it to Tim.

"Okay?" said Tim. "We'll insert it. You watch."

"I'm avid. Insert away, Angel, and drink up!"

Tim cheerfully quaffed his glass, Peggy took it, refilled it and handed it back and raised hers. "Here's to angels!" she announced. "They fly in from the most unexpected places!"

"Yeah, don't they just." Tim crouched before the television, Peggy close beside him.

"Look at all the pretty little lights!" cried Peggy. "It's Christmas already!"

"Now," said Tim. "Watch. I take the cassette...and insert it real slow so's you can see. Yeah?"

"Yeah! Let's manoeuvre!" cried Peggy who knew she was far merrier than she ought to be.

Tim slowly inserted the videocassette. Peggy's eyes were on him, particularly his delicious rear as he crouched -- that patch of exposed skin jut below his shirt, where his lower back had begun to divide into two healthy buttocks. Tim knew she was watching only him and he made the most of it, intoning his voice importantly. "It's real easy. Now you do it." He turned to her, said seriously, "See? The telly's got to be on too. You got to have the telly on too, don't you?"

"Apparently," replied Peggy, looking deep into his fine blue-green eyes as he ejected the cassette and handed it to her.

"Now you do it. Slow. Real slow. Or the mechanism will reject it. You got to do it slow, don't you?"

"Yeah," said Peggy. "Or be rejected by the mechanism."

"You can't force it, can you?"

"Oh no. Wouldn't want to force it. Never force mechanisms. It could be dangerous."

Peggy inserted the cassette. It snapped in with a loud thud that made her jump yet closer to Tim. "Oh, Angel!" she said, leaning into his side. "Have I done something wrong? Did I break it?"

"Nah," said Tim. "Not at all. Okay so far?"

"Roger," said Peggy.

"Okay. This is the play button. See? Play. Right? Yeah?"

"Right. Yeah," said Peggy, "You got to hit all the right buttons, don't you?"

Peggy, thought Peggy, what on earth are you up to? What are you playing at? Her eyes on Tim, Peggy froze.

"Well you got to push it, don't you?" said Tim, grinning that grin. "It don't play if you don't push it, does it?"

Peggy pushed the 'play' button. Young, handsome Willy came on the large television screen. Peggy was rapt, forgot Tim, blue-green eyes, butt and all. But Tim's interest in Peggy was fully aroused. He quaffed his drink and boldly watched her kneeling before the TV. He poured himself another at Willy's bar, returned and sat gazing at Peggy who was glued to swimming-suited Willy as he rose from the lawn of a tiny, enclosed garden and ambled, smiling, toward the camera.

"That's my angel, Angel," said Peggy over her shoulder, sipping scotch. "That's my Willy! Hello, Willy!"

Willy's face loomed large on the screen. His mouth moved, slowly, silently forming 'I love you, Peggeen.'

Without turning from the screen Peggy said "Christ! Isn't he beautiful?!"

Tim had moved closer to Peggy, said "Yeah."

"We were children -- kids when we married."

"Yeah."

"That's our garden. See?" Peggy gestured nonchalantly toward the study window. "Our garden. It's still back there. We sunbathed there in our garden. Still do... Did."

Peggy giggled at her video Willy who was now marching about in his swimsuit flexing his muscles like some comic-book strongman. She giggled and held her empty glass out for a refill, thought again: what am I playing at? -- but knew, had known from the start of her little escapade. Although the speed with which it was proceeding took her breath away and made her heart pound.

Tim filled the glass from a full bottle he'd brought from the bar. "Tah, love," she said, still admiring her clowning Willy. "Isn't he bee-uu-ti-ful?!"

"Yeah," said Tim who finished his own glass and happily poured himself another.

"Hello, Willy!" cried Peggy, yet again. "We're watching you!" Without taking her eyes from Willy she announced "Willy is my angel! We were each other's angels for twenty years. I bought him that swimsuit. Suits him!" She laughed at her little pun. "Tell me, Tim," she said, her eyes still riveted to the TV screen, "don't you think it suits him?!"

"Yeah," said Tim.

The video Willy did an excellent somersault on the tiny lawn. Peggy giggled, splashing her drink.

"You got any kids?" said Tim.

Turning to him at last, Peggy said "Only you, Angel. Willy didn't want kids. Willy didn't need kids. He had me. I was Willy's angel." Peggy suddenly grabbed Tim's hand, jerked him close to the television screen, cried "Watch this!"

Willy, who was now very close to the camera, suddenly turned, dropped his swimsuit and flashed his buttocks. Peggy laughed raucously, jumped up from the floor and threw herself into Willy's chair and screamed, "He's mooning us! Mooning us! He's an angel! We're all sodding, mooning angels, aren't we? God bless us! God bloody bless us all! You're an angel too, Tim! For bringing my Willy back to me!"

"Bringing him back? I thought you said he was out for the evening?"

"He is. Out for several evenings. A millennium of evenings. And then some."

"Huh?"

Peggy was about to answer but stopped short, gasped as

she saw Willy walking toward a very pretty woman. It was the young Margaret.

"The part that's coming up is revolting. Some whore got loose in our garden. Some demented bachelor joke. Jack was behind it -- you don't know Jack. I hope you didn't watch it when you taped it. It's disgusting. I hope you..."

"No, I didn't, Missus. It was private."

"Good! Can we rewind? I want to see...Please! Stop this machine now!"

Tim pressed the rewind button. Peggy watched closely as the picture raced backwards.

"We're moving back in time! A miracle!" said Peggy, relieved. Could Tim see that? That he was witnessing a miracle, her miracle? Yes, he could.

"Bein' on the technical side myself, I believe you can safely say that. Video sure is some kind of miracle of modern technology."

The rewind stopped with a loud click and the screen went blank. Tim pushed another button.

"See? I actuated the power-on switch again. Did you note the auto-stop function after rewind?"

"Yeah," said Peggy, wondering if she had an auto-stop function too. "Duly noted. I'll drink to that!"

Peggy raised her glass to Tim who raised his and kneeled beside her. They clicked glasses and drank and he 'actuated' the video player. Peggy grinned affectionately at Tim for a moment but returned her attention to the video when her swim-suited Willy appeared. "Isn't he beautiful? Oh, look Tim! Oh! He's going to be naughty again!" Peggy took a quick swallow, set down her glass and clapped her hands. "Here it comes!" The Video-Willy turned, dropped his swimsuit, bared his buttocks. Peggy giggled and suddenly grabbed Tim. She planted a long, urgent kiss on his lips then broke away and cried. "You do that, Angel! Like Willy! Flip us your bottom! Moon us, Angel!"

Tim drained his glass, tossed it on the carpet. He jumped up from his knees, turned and dropped his trousers and bared his buttocks. Peggy stopped laughing. "Turn off the goddamned video!" she screamed.

Tim pulled up his trousers, zipped his fly and swayed tipsily above her. Peggy was silent, glared up at him.

"Missus?" said Tim.

"Turn off these goddamned machines and please do not call me Missus!"

Tim, hurt and angry, obediently switched off the video and television and tramped furiously to the front door without looking at Peggy. His hand was on the latch as she shouted "Stay with me! Please, Tim! Stay with me!"

He froze at the door. He was a good man but he was humiliated. He could not bear to turn and face Peggy.

"Stay with me," she pleaded. "Willy won't be home tonight. Stay with me. Please, Tim."

Tim turned, swayed from the door, regarded Peggy silently. He was not her fucking toy-boy! She was nothing to him! For God's sake he'd only just met the woman! She had no right to speak to him like that! But she had begun to cry. She was huddling on that nice, expensive rug and cryin' her poor heart out. Although he was no knight in shining armour he was a gentleman. He forgot his own hurt, his own humiliation. What was that to Peggeen's pain? She was crying. He knew how that felt -- to want, to need something important real bad. Real, real bad and not to have it. So he said softly, as softly as he could, "Peggeen?"

She watched him helplessly through her tears. She was not a person who enjoyed appearing helpless, hated herself for it and tried hard to smile. He was a very kind man and, as very kind men cry easily, he began to cry.

Tim was asleep in the large double bed, the nicest bed he had ever seen in the nicest bedroom he had ever been in.

Peggy lay restlessly awake beside him. Feeling old, guilty and lost, she studied the familiar cracks in the dimly lit ceiling of hers and Willy's bedroom. The ceiling had needed paint for several years but there was comfort in it. It was an old and imperfect friend. Like Margaret, it was known. After a moment, as quietly as she could, she pulled herself up and slipped out of bed and threw Willy's dressing gown over her nakedness. Careful not to wake Tim, she crept out of the bedroom and down the stairs.

In the kitchen she filled a kettle, put it on and took out a tin of tea. As before, she set a tray for two but swore and snatched back one cup and cast it violently into the sink where it shattered. She stumbled for a moment, catching her balance with both hands on the kitchen counter then, steadied, switched on the television and video, managed to rewind the videocassette and started it.

Peggy allowed the cassette to proceed to where Willy's lips silently said 'I love you, Peggeen'. The kettle whistled and Peggy fetched in her tea, set it carefully by her chair and, in the study, took one of Willy's pipes from its rack. She filled, tamped, and lit it and puffed away, all the while laughing at Willy's clownish antics which she rewound and played again and again, stopping each time before Willy, having dropped his swimsuit and mooned, turned toward the young, beautiful Margaret. With a start Peggy became aware of Tim in his underpants, watching her incredulously from the staircase. She took Willy's smoking pipe from her lips, smiled and motioned him to sit and said "Tea, Angel?"

"I wouldn't say no," he said, yawning. "What time is it?"

"Middle of the night time, Angel."

"I got to work tomorrow."

"I got tea. You want tea?"

"Yeah," said Tim. "Please."

Peggy returned to the kitchen as Tim sat watching Willy bare his buttocks and Peggy called, "Has he flashed his bottom yet?"

"Yeah. Just now."

"I like bottoms, don't you?" called Peggy. "Could you rewind, please? Before the bit with the hired whore?"

"Yeah," said Tim and pressed the rewind button as Peggy entered with a cup of tea and a dish of biscuits, sat and said "Milk?"

"I wouldn't say no."

Peggy splashed milk into the cup, poured tea, and held up a delicate little sugar bowl.

"How many?" she asked.

"Lots, please."

Peggy added several teaspoonfuls of sugar.

"Tah," said Tim, stirring his sugary tea.

The video finished its rewind and clicked off.

"Note how it turns itself off automatically?" said Tim.

"Yeah. I noted that. I wish I could."

"Could what?" asked Tim.

"I wish I could turn myself off. Perhaps I shall," said Peggy, stirring her tea with an exquisite little silver spoon.

"You're nice," said Tim.

"Am I?"

"Yeah."

"Say it again."

"You're real nice." Tim stood up beside her in his underpants and stretched, leaving nothing to Peggy's imagination. He sat on the floor by her, said "tea's nice."

"Good."

"Can I always call you Peggeen?"

"No, love. That was...special."

"Well you're real nice anyhow, anyhow."

"We both are, Angel."

"Your husband nice?"

"Yeah."

"He don't beat you or nothin'?" said Tim with a wicked

smile.

"He should," said Peggy.

"He looks nice."

Peggy nodded, sipped her tea. Tim began to eat a biscuit, and speaking through it, said "Nice. Make 'em yourself?"

"Yeah," said Peggy who obviously hadn't -- their open package lay on the tray beside them. "Willy calls biscuits, cookies. He's American."

"Nice," said Tim and thrust his bare legs fetchingly before him on that nice rug.

Peggy set down her tea with a great clunk. "Look. I'm tired of bobbing up and down switching this video thingy backward and forward. I want Willy at the tip of my fingers. Isn't there something easier?"

Tim jumped up and, eager to please, took a small remote from the TV carton.

"You got a remote too. Actuates the telly and the video both. I was going to show you how it works before but... we got sidetracked."

Tim grinned at Peggy and held up the remote. "It actuates everything, you see. Only you hold it in your hand, like. All the functions are the same, like.

Peggy held the control in her hand, said suddenly "I've got a little cassette. Just sound. Willy speaks to me. He says..."

"He says I love you, Peggeen."

"How did you know that?"

"He says it on the film don't he, Willy? And he's overdoin' it, ain't he? You want me to lip-sync the tape to this video, don't you?"

"Can you, Angel?"

"Sure. I got to go now. Got to get up early." Tim drained his cup, stuffed the last 'cookie' into his mouth and sprang up. Suddenly remembering he was in his underpants, he covered his crotch with both hands and laughed. But Peggy was taking an audiocassette from Willy's desk drawer and didn't see him.

"It's at the beginning." She handed the cassette to Tim. "Willy says 'I love you, Peggeen' three times. Use the last one. It's the loudest. I want to hear it all over the goddamned house."

"Yeah."

"Can you make the picture and the sound repeat over and over again so I don't have to switch it back and forth to see it again?"

"Yeah. How many times?"

"Six? No. Ten. Ten times. 'I love *you*, Peggeen', ten times."

"Sure. Ten times. I love you."

"I love *you*, Peggeen!" corrected Peggy.

"Yeah. I gotta go," said Tim.

Tim ejected the videocassette from the video player.

"Wait!" cried Peggy. "Don't take that. I want to play it tonight. I...need to..."

Peggy took the film reel from the sofa where she'd flung it.

"Use this film again. Be careful. It crumbles."

"Yeah. I know."

"The tape, Tim... don't listen to all of it. Please, love. The part I want is at the beginning. I wouldn't want anybody to hear all of it. They might think...they might think all was not well with Willy and me when it was. Know what I mean? We played games, Willy and I. We weren't always ourselves on the tapes. Know what I mean? We weren't always serious. It was games. When we argued -- only games."

"Sure," said Tim. It was games. We all play games sometimes. Look. I got to go."

"Of course."

Tim ran up the stairs to dress. Peggy took a sip of tea. It was cold. The telephone rang. She looked at her watch, frowned, allowed it to ring on. After several rings it stopped. Tim stood in the study doorway watching Peggy. He caught her eye and grinned the grin he had grinned in the television shop. Peggy said "I didn't recognize you with your clothes on."

Tim thought this hugely funny and laughed. Peggy smiled

only slightly, took the audiocassette and the old film reel from the top of the television and shivered as she laid them in his hand. She tried to appear calm and nonchalantly attempted a sip of cold tea but her hands shook so badly the cup rattled. The more she tried to steady herself, the more she shook. Some awful, delayed reaction overpowered her, pushing aside the anger that had held sorrow at bay and sustained her.

Tim set down the film reel and the audiocassette and rushed to Peggy. With ineffable tenderness he took the rattling cup and saucer from her and kissed Peggy's shaking hands. She began to sob and fell gracelessly into Willy's reading chair. Tim kneeled beside her, pulled Willy's loose dressing gown gently around her and tucked her into it and hugged her and rocked her back and forth in his arms. "It's all right, Peggeen," he whispered. "It's all right, love."

In Willy's study the next day, in his dressing gown, Willy's unlit pipe in her mouth, and a jumble of audiocassettes in her lap, sat Peggy at Willy's desk. Sipping coffee and munching toast she listened, entranced, to her cassette recorder.

> "For God's sake, Willy!"
> "You are a cow, Peggy!"
> "Go to Hell!"
> "Come back here, Peggeen!"

Margaret crept stealthily down the steps into the little entrance garden and slipped a key into Peggy's door, inched it quietly open and entered. She immediately spied Peggy and tip-toed to the open study door and shrieked "Good morning!"

Willy's pipe fell from Peggy's mouth and the audiocassettes tumbled from her lap as she jumped up. "How the hell did you get in?!" she screamed.

"So you're still about?! Liar!"

"So it seems!"

"Better get to Yorkshire before the old hag drops dead!" cried Margaret.

"Who?!"

"Willy's ancient aunt. Liar. Turn off that cassette. It's lies! All lies!"

Peggy increased the volume on the player and aimed the speaker directly at Margaret.

"Get out, whore!" cried Peggy. "Give me that key and get your drunken arse out of Willy's house!"

"Willy didn't have any aunts! Liar!"

"He did. Give me that key. She's ninety-four. Where did you get that key?!"

"You said she was ninety-nine!"

"She's a hundred and one if she's a day. Give me that key and get out of my house. Where did you get that fucking key?!"

"Willy gave it to me."

"Oh Christ! So you fucked here too! Begone, strumpet!"

"You know very well we met here, Peggy. You left on several occasions, expressly so we could meet here. You left to meet someone. God only knows who it was. I suspect it was Jack. Or was it that other doctor trying to curry favour with famous Dr Willy's wife? What were you doing with Willy's pipe?"

Peggy glared venomously at Margaret, grabbed Willy's pipe from where it had fallen, stuck it in her mouth, lit it and began to puff.

"My God! What are you doing?!"

"Smoking."

"You don't smoke."

"Do. Only pipes."

"Liar. I never saw you smoke."

"Jesus Christ! There was life-before-Margaret! You don't know everything."

"Almost. Don't call me Margaret. Have you been drinking?"

"No. Have you?"

"At nine in the morning?"

"Do forgive me. I thought it was nine-fifteen," snapped Peggy.

Margaret sat with a grunt in Willy's reading chair.

"Did I give you permission to sit?" said Peggy, "Do not sit down! You are not welcome. You are not allowed to stay." Peggy turned up the volume on the little audiocassette player:

> "Peg! Peggeen, darling! It was all her fault! We'd had a bit too much, you know how that is, and she just grabbed me! Then and there! Margaret just grabbed me!"

"Liar!" screamed Margaret and sat up sharply, "Will you turn that damned cassette off? You put Willy up to that."

Peggy switched off the player.

"Thank you!" said Margaret, "Oh, Peggy, I miss him so."

"Me too," said Peggy, chewing.

"What are you eating?"

"Toast."

"Why don't we go out for breakfast?"

"I'm having breakfast."

"I'm starving, whined Margaret. "I walked all the way from Victoria bloody station. Give me some."

"I do not breakfast with whores."

"I'll take you to lunch," said Margaret, dabbing at an eye with her huge hanky and simultaneously scratching at an ankle.

"You can't afford it."

"No, I can't," agreed Margaret.

"If you took me out to lunch," said Peggy, "it would cost you more than a bottle of, what is that stuff you drink?"

"Bourbon. 'Four Roses'," said Margaret, dabbing at her

other eye.

"Your nose looks like Four Roses in a hairnet," said Peggy, "all veiny and red."

"It is American bourbon whisky. Willy favoured it. And I favour it."

"It does not favour you, you penniless alcoholic!"

"When I want your opinion I'll ask for it!" said Margaret.

"No you won't. Because you will not be here. Get out!" cried Peggy, and rose menacingly from Willy's desk.

"When I want your opinion," repeated Margaret, nonchalantly scratching at her other ankle. "I'll ask for it."

"May I have that in writing?" said Peggy, "In a letter? Preferably posted from a great distance?"

"Why don't you take me to lunch?" sighed Margaret.

"No," said Peggy, who sat again and stuffed in a large bite of toast and butter and mumbled through it. "I'm having breakfast."

"Fetch me some. I'm your oldest friend, Peggy, doesn't that count for something?"

"Your advanced age has nothing to do with it, Margaret."

"Willy met me first, almost married me. And he might have. Later of course. After he'd divorced you."

"Willy didn't marry you because of your chequered past. Or was it your chequered nose? He always said your nose looked like the four roses on your bourbon bottles. Tied in a hairnet."

"Liar!"

"I'm only repeating what Willy said."

"And you're a liar!"

"And you're a rosey-nosed whore. I have it on tape. Straight from Willy's cupid's bow lips."

"We know about your tapes, Peggy-liar."

"Get out, Margaret. I've got to pee."

"No, you don't. You just don't want to talk to me. That's it, isn't it?"

Peggy laughed. "It had entered my mind."

"Jean says you always have to pee!" hissed Margaret.

"It's those yeast infections, dear, those yeast infections you gave us, one and all."

"Trichomoniasis! *Trichomoniasis!*" screamed Margaret. "Willy never got it from me! You got it from Jack and gave to Willy who gave it to me!"

"And Jack got it from Jean?" said Peggy and laughed again, what she hoped was an exceedingly cruel laugh.

"Pooh! Jean wouldn't touch a fly."

"If the hypocritical cow had stuck to flies she wouldn't have got trichomoniasis! "

"Pooh on Jean," said Margaret. "God, I'm hungry."

"Jean. The hypocritical cow."

"Pooh on Jean," said Margaret. "We were simply experimental. All of us. It was the thing wasn't it? It was the thing to do. We were modern."

The two women regarded one another solemnly for a moment and began to titter then laughed. Peggy stopped laughing. "I've got to pee. Go away. Go home and powder your rosy nose. Take a bath for chrissake!"

Peggy banged down her coffee cup and slammed herself into the little loo off the hall.

"I might have known you'd pee sooner or later," said Margaret and picked up a piece of Peggy's toast, munched, washed it down with coffee, hollered "Your coffee is cold!" She shuffled idly through the tumbled pile of audiocassettes Peggy had been sorting. "Where were you last night about two a.m.? I rang you."

Peggy squatted sullenly on the toilet, frowned for a moment then smiled.

"Where were you?" demanded Margaret. "You're always awake at two. Where were you?"

"Peeing!" shouted Peggy through the door.

"Liar. Where were you?"

"Entertaining a young friend."

"Liar," said Margaret, "My God! You do take a long time in there!"

Margaret nosed through a few more cassettes and wandered to the videocassette player and pressed the eject button. With a noisy clatter, Peggy's new videocassette shot out.

"Keep your whorish fingers off my memento mori!" cried Peggy through the loo door. The toilet flushed and Peggy rushed out, snatched her new videocassette from Margaret. "You've had your fun," she cried. "Now get out!"

"Sweet Jesus!" said Margaret. "A telly! A video! My God. You're well-equipt!"

"So is he!"

"Who?! Who is well-equipt?!"

Peggy held out her hand. "Key. You've no right to that key. Give me that key."

"No. Not till I've seen your videocassette," said Margaret.

"Jesus, for a whore, you're a pushy hag! Now give me that key."

"Not till I've seen your videocassette, you cruel bitch." Margaret snatched the cassette from Peggy and backed away kicking a chair between them.

"Give me my videocassette!" Peggy moved menacingly toward Margaret with fire in her eyes.

"You will not have your cassette until I have seen it."

The women slowly circled the chair. Margaret gave up, handed the cassette to Peggy.

Peggy held out her other hand. "Key!" she demanded.

Margaret took the key from her jacket pocket, dropped it in Peggy's outstretched hand, said "Oh, Peggy. I miss him so."

"Who doesn't?" whispered Peggy.

"I'll ring you this afternoon?" said Margaret.

"I'll be in Yorkshire!"

"Liar," said Margaret, moving slowly to the door. "You'll be all right?"

Peggy was silent, glowered at Margaret who stood sadly in the doorway.

"Peggy? You'll be all right?"

Peggy did not answer.

"Peggy! Will you be all right?! You worry me, you --"

Peggy gave Margaret a push and closed the door in her face. Margaret lingered outside for a moment -- would Peggy open the door again and let her in and give her breakfast? No. Muttering to herself, Margaret turned and walked away. Peggy, behind her door, shuddered, pulled Willy's dressing gown closer, and hurried back to her television and video player. She sat in Willy's old reading chair which had now become, miraculously, Peggeen's very own television chair. She very competently inserted the videocassette and 'actuated' it and sat, mesmerized.

> Young, remarkably handsome, Willy, in his revealing swimming suit, now headed for the young beautiful Margaret who, a tall drink in her hand, sat alone at a garden table, a bottle of Four Roses bourbon whiskey beside her.

"Meet Maggie," announced Peggy to the empty room. "Maggie, hired whore."

> Young Willy chased the beautiful young Margaret in circles around the small back garden. Suddenly, an older Willy turned from his study desk and frowned into the camera which he motioned away. But the camera pursued him, came in very close, teasing. He jumped up and pursued the now bumpily retreating camera. A small

enclosed garden appeared, decorated for a party. An older Margaret smiled for the camera and poured a drink, holding up for the camera her bottle of 'Four Roses' bourbon. She smiled and Willy moved in, grabbed the bottle from her and drank from it. Margaret attempted in vain to retrieve the bottle, while behind her, an older couple, Jean and Jack, cavorted, pseudo-erotically for the camera. Margaret's bottle dropped and shattered on the garden tiles. The older Margaret, caught in merciless close-up, swayed over the bottle, staggered and dropped awkwardly into a garden chair. She attempted to avoid another intimidating close-up and hid her face in her hands. Several black frames appeared. Then, half-hidden by a large fern, Willy and Margaret embraced.

"Bitch!" screamed the widow Peggy. "Bitch!"

The camera veered radically and moved around the fern and peered up Margaret's skirt. Suddenly, full-screen, a much older Willy's sleeping face appeared.

Peggy studied this far older sleeping Willy longingly for a moment, slipped slowly from Willy's chair and crawled on her knees to the television screen and pressed her face against it.

Peggy was frightened from her reverie as the telephone rang. She tried to switch off the video but fumbled the buttons. The abhorrent scenes of Willy and Margaret hurtled crazily back and forth at high speed. Panicked, she switched off the video and snatched up the ringing telephone but did not speak.

"Peggy? Is that you?" said Jean.

"Possibly. Who wants to know?"

"Jean wants to know, love. You were supposed to ring me."

"Was I?"

"You promised," persisted Jean.

"I'm a liar, Jeanie. Shoot me at dawn."

"We nearly came to visit you, Jack and I, last night."

"Close call, that," stage-whispered Peggy.

Jean ignored her, said "Well. I thought we could, you and I, since you are here, have lunch. I've got the car today. I can pick you up."

"Jeanie?"

"Yes, dear?" Jean's brow automatically furrowed -- something unpleasant was coming. She knew that tone of voice.

"Do you remember Willy ever taking movies of me? I haven't been able to find any. I've searched, Jeanie, dear. But in vain. Why didn't Willy take moving pictures of me? *Me*, whom he professed to love."

"You wouldn't let him, dear."

"Why?"

"Don't ask me."

"Why not? You're my friend, aren't you, Jeanie?"

"Well. Of course, I'm your friend."

"Why didn't my Willy take pictures of me, whom he professed to love?"

"Well. I don't know, do I?"

"Apparently not. Friendship does indeed seem to have its limits, don't it?"

"What?"

"Nothin'."

"In any case, Peggy, it was your camera, wasn't it? You always made that abundantly clear."

"Why didn't Willy just force the camera away from me and

take over? Didn't he want moving pictures of me? Was I so unattractive?"

"Well. Now that I think of it. You wouldn't let a camera near you. Do not ask me why for I do not know. Peggy, you do forget!"

"I can't even remember what I looked like. What did I look like?"

"Well. Just as you look now. Younger, of course."

"Cold comfort," sighed Peggy.

"Really, you are are silly."

"Was I as pretty as Willy, Jeanie?"

Jean was silent. Where was this all going?

Precisely as before, Peggy said, "was I as pretty as Willy, Jeanie?"

"Men are not pretty, Peggy. Men are...well. Men are rugged."

"What was I then? Petite? Comely? A horse's arse?!"

"Everybody envied you! You had Willy, didn't you?! Really. You are a big silly!"

"Only after funerals," whispered Peggy.

"I didn't mean...Peggy, I'm sorry."

"Don't be. Just because someone dies doesn't make him a goddamned saint!"

Jean frowned, plucked a bit of lint from her sleeve, scrutinized her Cartier. "Well. No lunch then?"

"No. I'm sorting out. Just a moment, please."

Peggy went to Willy's study, took his revolver from its drawer and returned to the telephone. She laid the revolver on the table beside her.

"There must be such a lot," said Jean, "a lot to sort out. I could help."

"No. There's not so much, really. Not nearly so much as I thought."

"Well. When do you leave?"

"Leave?"

"Yorkshire, dear. You said you were going to Yorkshire."

"When I'm sorted out I'll leave. Instantly." Peggy took up Willy's revolver, pressed it to her cheek.

"Shall I ring you tomorrow?"

"Yes. Do. If you dare."

"Well. I must say, I'm relieved. The old Peggy. You do sound better."

"Jean?"

"Yes, dear?"

"Did you like Willy's Poems?"

"They were excellent."

"Really?!"

"Oh yes. Both Jack and I always thought so. Willy was so very sensitive."

"Was he?!" gasped Peggy.

"Who would know better than you, dear? You read Literature, didn't you? In some dusty Oxbridge corridor?"

"I did?! My God, I'd forgotten!"

"Well. You never let us mere mortals forget it."

"Was I a monster?"

"No more than anyone who always got precisely what she wanted. Perhaps you were a monsterette," laughed Jean. "I'm not complaining, Peggy, neither is Jack. Well. If there's to be no lunch today, this granny must run. Marcia's little Jenny. Birthday number two tomorrow!"

"No!" cried Peggy

"Yes! Inconceivable, isn't it? Byeeee!"

"Byeeee, Granny!"

Peggy leaned back, whispered "Granny" once more and rose, found a book, returned to Willy's chair, whispered "Granny" again and began to read with only the occasional glance at Willy's gun, tight beside her.

Evening had come and certain lamps, after much rearranging, were strategically placed around the room. Peggy was dressed to kill. At Willy's chic little bar, she set out a fine crystal decanter of scotch, and two heavy, cut-crystal glasses. The telephone rang, she lifted the receiver. "Yeah?" she said, Tim's perfect grin turning pleasantly in her head.

"Good evening! Did I tell you that John Lennon has been shot?"

"You did. They're dropping like flies," said Peggy.

"That was a rather flip remark for a fallen icon," slurred Margaret.

Peggy was silent.

"What're you doing? Besides not going to Yorkshire? Liar. God! You'd think Yorkshire was the end of the world, the way you're not going to it! What're you doing then, besides lapping up all of Willy's Black Label?"

"That's your bag, Mags. As for the grieving Peggeen, here she is waiting for her gentleman caller, dressed to the nines, eyelids drooping under a pound of green shadow."

"Pooh!" said Margaret, "Green's out, mauve's in."

"So are gentleman callers."

"Pooh. What're you wearing?"

"What are you, a pervert?" snapped Peggy.

Margaret brought a glass to her mouth, sipped noisily, set it down. "What're you wearing?"

"That purple, green-fringed, flapper thing that I wore for the last Charleston resurrection. It still fits."

"Liar."

"Goes with my unfashionable green eyelids."

"Liar."

"Margaret, you are brimful of je ne sais quoi!"

"What, precisely do you mean by that, Miss know-it-all?"

"Let's just leave it at 'brimful', smiled Peggy, jumping as the doorbell rang. "Voila! He's here!"

"Liar."

"Byeeee!" sang Peggy. She slammed down the telephone and rushed to the door. It was Tim, and delicious grin fixed, he handed her the precious videocassette and the old film reel.

"Come in, Angel," said Peggy who caught her breath as she caught his grin. But now, Tim hesitated, the grin vanished. He seemed apprehensive.

"Come in, Angel!" she said again and dropped the old film on Willy's bar and kissed the videocassette and placed it carefully by the television.

"Sit." Peggy motioned to a chair, "Sit, Angel."

He sat. Peggy poured a whisky for both of them, handed one to him and sat opposite in Willy's reading chair, sang "Cheers!"

Tim half heartedly lifted his glass, sighed "Yeah."

"What's up, Angel? Everything all right?"

"Yeah. Sure. Been going all right for you, then?"

"I'm bored shitless. Been reading. All day. James."

"James who?" said Tim, eyes cast down.

"Henry James. 'Portrait of a Lady'."

"What's she do then? The lady?" said Tim, looking as though he was about to cry.

"What does she do? She suffers, that's what! She's a professional fucking martyr."

"I didn't know they had those."

"She wants to suffer. It's delicious. She enjoys it."

"Weird."

"Actually. She's a sanctimonious, selfish little bitch."

"Yeah?"

"Yeah."

He wasn't Tim tonight. Something was wrong. He was suffering. He would not be allowed to suffer -- no matter what the reason. She would comfort him as he had comforted her. "What is it, Angel? You must tell me."

"My Angela's gone and left me. Sussed I was with you last night and she left me."

"The selfish little...! Angel, you need a drink!"

Tim held up his glass. "I already got one, thanks."

"Quaff it, love. I'll pour you another. You'll never get old if you don't drink."

Tim downed his drink. Peggy downed her own and poured them each another.

"Gimme Angela's number and I'll ring her for you."

"She ain't home. She's out with Larry."

"Who the fuck is Larry?!"

Tim stuck a finger in his drink, stirred it sadly. "Larry's my boss. He's got a future."

"Who sez?"

"Angela says," said Tim, miserably.

"A future is unavoidable, my darling. Whatever Angela says. Your Angela is a wee bit soft in her noggin."

"Oh Angela's all right, all right. We just don't see eye to eye, her and me, anymore. Larry's okay too. How 'bout some music then?"

"Help yourself." Peggy led Tim to Willy's record collection.

Tim spotted the Sibelius record on the bookcase. "Si-bee-lee-us. Who're they then?"

"I don't know. It was Willy's," said Peggy.

Tim slipped the record out of its sleeve, saw the knife-slash Peggy has inflicted.

"Your Willy. He's dead, ain't he?"

"Probably."

Tim browsed through the records.

"Not to your taste?" said Peggy,

"Bar-tok," said Tim. "Who're they then?"

"Forget the records, Angel. We'll hum to one another."

Tim ambled over to sit on the floor beside Peggy who now sprawled in Willy's reading chair.

"He didn't know much about music, did he?"

"No. But he was a looker," said Peggy.

"Huh?"

"He...was...beautiful."

"You're not so bad yourself, Missus," said Tim, brightening

somewhat.

"Nobody ever noticed me," said Peggy. "Not when I was with Willy. Not even the men. Even the men looked at Willy before they looked at me."

"He wasn't...?" Tim made a gesture, not sarcastic, informative.

"Don't I wish," said Peggy, "I might have seen more of him." She laughed. Tim laughed with her, not knowing what she meant, but only because he liked her. She was sad too. Like him. But she was funny. When he was sad he couldn't be funny. Not at all. Not even if he tried hard. Everything showed. He couldn't hide it. Not even if he tried hard.

"Willy was buried, I mean burnt, two days ago," said Peggy, "I've been a bit mad. Mental. I've been drinking too much. I've never liked alcohol. But it's the drug of choice for my generation. I actually hate the stuff. I've been a monster. I've not been... kind."

"I thought it was something like that." He patted her hand gently. He was a kind man, Peggy knew, this comforter of hers.

"So what'll you do now?" said Peggy. "About Angela."

"It's pretty much up to Angela. She's got a mind of her own."

"Lucky Angela." Peggy thought poor Tim would soon begin to cry. Not like Margaret, or Peggy herself. But like a man. As a man would cry -- going very pink, squinching his eyes, turning away, embarrassed, when the tears came. Ashamed of the tears. A beautiful man. Tim's grin made him beautiful. It was indisputable. Crying would make him glorious.

Peggy took the new videocassette from its box. "How'd our lip-sync go?"

"Great," he said. He was feeling much better now. "Want to play it?"

"Doesn't it bother you that Angela's out with Larry?!" cried Peggy angrily, out of nowhere. Tim stared at her. "Don't you care a damn," cried Peggy. "Don't you care a damn what they're doing this very fucking minute?!"

Tim was confused. He clasped her hand, began to pull her toward him. She did not draw away, only slowly shook her head. Dismayed, he stopped.

"Angels are a comfort, Tim. You're a very special angel. But us widows got long memories. I'm so sorry, darling. You'd better go."

Tim was perplexed.

"You're very special, darling," she said again, softly. "Angela doesn't know her arse from a hole in the ground."

Tim forced a smile, was about to say thank you for calling him very special but he didn't. He wasn't sure it was the right thing to say. Peggy took some money from her purse, offered it to him. He refused.

"Come now, love," said Peggy. "That's not fair." She held up the videocassette. "These things cost money and time."

"You can give me that book," said Tim. The lady's portrait? I'll read it. Maybe we can get together later, huh? Talk about it? I don't read much. I should read better. Maybe we can get together?"

"Yeah," said Peggy. "Maybe we can, love."

Peggy took the book from Willy's reading table, handed it to Tim and lead him to the door. As he passed her he turned quickly and kissed her on the cheek. She shut the door, stood for a moment listened to Tim get into his car and drive away. Tim was a good man, a kind and gentle man. A gentleman.

Peggy pressed the videocassette to her face.

"You're not going anywhere tonight, are you, Willy?"

Peggy went to Willy's desk, took out Willy's revolver and a few bullets and returned to Willy's reading chair where she sat and clicked open the revolver's chamber. She replaced all its bullets, snapped it shut and laid it on the table beside her. She inserted the videocassette into the player and switched on the television. Her young Willy, smiling in his swimsuit, appeared and ambled, much as youngish Tim had ambled just now, grinning, toward her. Peggy herself grinned at what might have been her very last thought and lifted Willy's revolver to her head and placed its muzzle against her temple.

"You'd better pee now, Peggeen!" screamed a very tipsy Margaret through the door. "Because I've got a few things to say to you!"

Peggy rushed to the study, hid Willy's revolver and returned to Willy's reading chair, before her new television. Suddenly, Margaret was pounding violently at the door. "Let me in!" she shrieked.

"Use your key!" cried Peggy.

"You took it! Let me in!"

"Piss off!" Peggy took a large swallow from Willy's favourite whisky glass.

"Goddamn you! Let me in!" screamed Margaret.

"You're nothing, Margaret! Nothing to me, nothing to Willy! You were always zero! You were nothing to Willy but a convenient screw!"

Peggy rose and watched from the little door window as Margaret stumbled back several feet and plunged toward the door. But Peggy flung it open, stepped aside and Margaret hurtled through, caught her toe in the elegant Persian rug and crashed to the floor. She lay there dazed, peering dully up at Peggy. "I loved Willy with all my heart," she whimpered at last. "Willy loved me." Margaret climbed from her knees and stood facing Peggy.

"Continue," said Peggy.

"I can't!" cried Margaret, "Not without Willy!"

"What's the alternative?!"

"To slit my throat! To snuff it!" screamed Margaret.

"That's viable," said Peggy, calmer.

"Don't think I'm serious. Do you? You don't think I'd do it."

"I don't much care either way," said Peggy.

"You cruel bitch. I'm serious about snuffing it."

"You'll do what suits you, Maggie. You always have," said Peggy.

"No, I have not! Never! I have never in my life done what I wanted!"

"Then you're a poor, deluded, alcoholic fool. You've no one to blame but yourself."

"I'm just like you, Peggy. I am you! And we both loved Willy!"

"Then we were both gullible fools!"

Margaret stumbled, leaned against a chair for support. Peggy backed away. Margaret swayed and mumbled and slowly began to lose her momentum. "You are a cow," she said. "I should have married somebody, anybody, just to lord it over you..."

"Nobody sane would marry a raving drunk."

"...Lord it over you just the way you've always lorded it over me. He loved me. And you are a cow. But..." continued Margaret, all anger somehow, instantly spent, "...But such a comfort."

Margaret reeled to a chair, fell into it and closed her eyes. "Your videocassette, Peggy. I want to see your bloody videocassette."

Peggy abruptly switched on the television and video and returned to her newly-minted television chair, as the smiling young Willy yanked down his swimming suit and bared his smooth, untanned bottom.

Margaret laughed sleepily, mumbled, "I remember that."

Peggy pressed rewind on her remote control until Willy's face appeared full screen and he grinned, grinned so like Tim, and Tim's face again turned in Peggy's head as young Willy said "I love *you*, Peggeen!"

"You did not, Willy," murmured Margaret drowsily from her chair. "You loved me."

Willy's grinning face, edited, jumped back full-screen. He spoke again. "I love *you*, Peggeen!"

"Liar!" sputtered Margaret at the edge of a snore.

Peggy rose silently and went quietly to Willy's desk, took out Willy's revolver.

"I love *you*, Peggeen!" said Willy for the third time, grinning from the television screen, precisely as before.

Grasping Willy's revolver in both hands, Peggy returned and sat in Willy's reading chair -- no! It was her chair! Her own goddamned television chair!

"I love *you*, Peggeen!" said Willy.

Peggy lifted the revolver.

Margaret awakened with a start from her doze and jerked upright. "He loved me!" she cried and began to scream as she saw the gun but stopped instantly when Peggy aimed it at her.

"I love *you*, Peggeen!" said Willy.

Margaret froze as Peggy aimed the gun at her own head.

"Peggy! Peggy! Don't!" she screamed.

"I love *you*, Peggeen!" said beautiful young Willy and Peggy turned the revolver toward him and closed her eyes and pulled the trigger and the television screen exploded.

Peggy dropped the gun and crumpled in her chair.

Margaret, terrified but suddenly oddly sober, after a moment, said "When?"

Peggy was silent then wearily turned her head -- who had spoken just now? There she was. It was pathetic Margaret sprawled there and shaking. Margaret, her oldest friend and fellow adulteress, attempting to move on -- just move on.

"When what?" asked Peggy.

"When are you...when... when are you going to Yorkshire?"

"Been, Maggie, been to Yorkshire. And returned."

"Oh, Peggy, I loved him so! I miss him so!"

"Yeah. Me too. Got to pee." Peggy rose, straightened her dress.

"But what about me?!" sobbed Margaret, "What about bloody me?!"

"Squat, Maggie. Nature does the rest."

Peggy disappeared into the loo and slammed the door. Margaret staggered to her feet and lurched, sobbing noisily, to Willy's study to riffle crazily through his books.

After several minutes, Peggy appeared, renewed, hair combed and fresh-faced after a quick splash, but most of all, oddly reassured by Margaret's familiarly frantic activity in Willy's study.

"May I have this?" mumbled Margaret, and held up the old framed photo of Willy she had just taken from his desk. "You've got the video, Peggy. May I have this?"

"Yeah. Sure you can, baby," said Peggy, mimicking Willy's American accent.

Margaret almost smiled and wobbling only slightly in her stocking feet, padded cautiously to Peggy who took her in her arms as Margaret, clutching Willy's picture, began, very softly, to cry. Peggy held her for a moment then led her gently up the stairs to the guest bedroom. Margaret attempted to speak but Peggy touched her own lips, made a sign of silence and Margaret obeyed.

Peggy helped Margaret to the bed where Margaret carefully laid Willy's framed photo on the bedside table, snorted once and was instantly asleep. Peggy covered her with a quilt, softly closed the door and started down the stairs.

In the study Peggy set Ravel's Piano Concerto in G on the turntable and carefully placed the tone arm at the second movement, the adagio. She went briskly to the kitchen, set the kettle on and returned to sit in Willy's...No! *her* chair, directly in front of the powdery ruin that remained of her new television. There she sat, immersing herself briefly in the lush, halting-waltz adagio of her favourite composer, then went to the kitchen, took a tray from the cupboard and was about to measure tea into the pot when she heard a voice.

"Peggeen?"

Peggy froze.

"Peggeen?"

The tea canister catapulted from Peggy's hand, went rolling across the kitchen floor. Peggy felt faint, retrieved the canister and steadied herself on the sideboard.

"Peggeen? Are you listening, darling?" said Willy.

Peggy dashed from the kitchen and gaped at the television which seemed to have acquired a new, silvery, shimmering screen upon which was Willy's serious face.

"Come closer, darling," he said.

Peggy, heart hammering crazily in her throat, went closer.

"Come a little closer, darling," said Willy, "so I can see you without my glasses."

Peggy moved closer and knelt before this television screen that simply could not be. This impossible television screen she had destroyed with Willy's gun only minutes before. Full-face on the screen in a close-up she, with her film camera, had no memory of, was her older Willy. He grinned at her, a magnificent grin she would never forget, and he said:

"I love *you*, Peggeen, my darling. I have never loved anyone in my life but my Peggeen."

Peggy gasped, caught her breath, whispered, "I love *you*, Willy, and I have never loved anyone but Willy."

"Do you forgive me, Peggeen?"

"Yes, Willy. But do you forgive me?"

"Of course I do, darling."

The kettle had been whistling for some time when Peggy returned to the kitchen and switched off the gas and took one cup from the cupboard.

HERBERT & AUBREY & ONDINE-NELLY

Herbert, fresh off a plane from California, had obviously stumbled upon one of those for-men-only London pubs where the "jolly old boys" gathered and wore their old school ties. How fortunate for me, he thought as he was clapped on the back and jostled happily up to a place at the bar, they think I'm one of them! How comforting to belong, if only for an evening! How comforting to forget ones woes amongst new found friends!

Herbert, who was to be briefly in London on business, had only the moment before resigned himself to a night of solitary drinking plagued by the painful recollection of recent loss. But all had now changed *in a twinkling,* Ondine-Nelly might sagely have observed. God! There she was, already destroying his new found bliss. There she was yet again, quoting one of her endless homilies. She had no business being there in his head -- not any more. She had left him for Mr Suggs. Herbert shook himself, ordered and downed in quick succession, six double whiskies and retreated to a far corner with his seventh.

Herbert was a relatively handsome man of about thirty-eight, though he could be and often was mistaken for even ten years younger. He had red hair, blue eyes, very regular features, beautiful white teeth which smiled nicely and often, was at least six feet tall and carried himself straight as a bayonet about which Ondine-Nelly had heartily approved... "Begone! Ondine-Nelly!" he muttered.

Ondine-Nelly, Herbert's fiancée of five years had only last week married a Mr Suggs about whom Herbert knew absolutely nothing. It had been "a bitter pill to swallow."

"Only a slut could do such a weirdo thing to a nice kid like you," said his grandmother who had immediately offered him a steaming cup of tea in which floated a tiny black ant struggling for life in a completely unexpected and disquieting environment. Which was precisely how Herbert felt. Like a black ant drowning in a cup of tea. Life without Ondine-Nelly was completely unexpected and, further, disquieting. So here he was in London, to forget Ondine-Nelly. To forget that misguided gorgeous girl.

When he had been here on an extended business trip the previous year she had peppered him with long tightly written letters containing encouraging messages: "A tended garden blooms forever!" and "Idle fingers play the Devil's lyre!"

He would now attempt to forget Ondine-Nelly and her Mr Suggs. But as he sipped his seventh scotch her voice sang in his head as it had when, in her church choir, she had sung in an unforgettable falsetto several beats behind her fellows, "JAY-ROOOOO-SALEM!" Herbert had been coerced into that front pew Sunday after Sunday by Ondine-Nelly's threats, in future, to keep her teeth tightly clenched when they kissed if he did not appear regularly in said pew. Why did he miss her? She was a monster! Well, no. He was the monster for thinking this!

"Anybody sitting here?"

Herbert looked up from his scotch and directly into the well-cared-for eyes of the slim young gentleman who had dropped into the seat beside him.

"Not to the best of my knowledge," said Herbert as the rippling image of Ondine-Nelly in her Sunday-best disappeared.

"How shall I put it?" said the young man, "I noticed that no one was sitting here with you and you seemed, apart from being obviously American, let's face it, how shall I put it, desperate?"

"Desperate?" said Herbert.

"So I decided to join you."

"To what?" asked Herbert.

"To join you!" repeated the young man.

"To join me to *what?*" asked Herbert, smiling uncertainly as his little joke, as always, misfired.

"Oh, I see," said the young man. "You were being funny."

"Sorry," said Herbert, with an unconvincing grin, "I was joking. I suppose I was trying to cheer myself up. I meant to facetiously imply that you wished to glue me, literally *attach* me to something."

"How about me attaching you to another drink?" said the slim young man, smiling, "That'll cheer you up."

"You thought I looked desperate?" asked Herbert.

"How shall I put this?" said the young man. "Let's face it, you didn't look happy."

"I was thinking of my ex-fiancée."

The young man smiled as he said "So you're not gay?"

"Not at all. I'm positively miserable!" said Herbert.

"Ill get you a drink, dear. What're you drinking?"

"Scotch and soda," said Herbert and thought -- as the young man made his way through the crowd of "jolly old boys" to the bar -- thought what an extremely friendly guy he was, but too young to be an "old boy". So what was he doing here in an "old boys" pub? Honestly, thought Herbert, if everyone was as friendly as this delightful young fellow there would be no need for wars. No need for men in uniform. Imagine -- thought Herbert and gulped and almost shed a tear because he was down-hearted to begin with -- imagine a world without war.

"A world without war!" exclaimed Ondine-Nelly the last time Herbert had seen her before the axe of Mr Suggs had fallen upon Herbert's tidy little five-year engagement and disquieted everything, "Would be a sorry place!" War, explained his Ondine-Nelly, brought out the noble nature in Man and fostered great scientific breakthroughs. Besides, she adored soldiers. And sailors. Men in uniform, she said, were definitely the "jewels in her crown."

Herbert did hope his ex-fiancée would be happy with her Mr Suggs. One simply did not associate with a woman for five whole years and subsequently wish her ill.

Herbert was feeling much better now as the three words, "a close escape" circled soothingly round his head. When the slim young man returned and placed a scotch and soda before him on the neat little Edwardian brass-topped table Herbert smiled graciously and toasted the slim young man who responded as he sat, with an affectionate pat on Herbert's knee and said: "How long have you been in London, love?"

"Hardly a day," said Herbert, noticing that this young man looked a bit older than he had originally surmised. "Are you an old boy?"

"Old enough to know better but too young to resist," whispered the relatively young man into Herbert's left ear and winked. "My name's Aubrey, what's yours?"

"Herbert."

"Welcome to London, Herbie!" whispered Aubrey, who patted Herbert's knee somewhat more affectionately than he had before and asked him to come home with him and have a coffee or whatever. Herbert accepted because he had already had seven double whiskies and the one just set before him would be his eighth and he was getting mighty sleepy and felt a coffee would wake him and the night was young. "Yes, said Herbert, a coffee would be just fine."

"Or whatever," whispered Aubrey and winked.

Herbert winked back but his eyelid stuck. He had never learned to wink properly in the first place and he felt a fool. He knew in his heart he was too drunk to care. But he did.

In their taxi, Aubrey's leg continually twitched up against Herbert's and Herbert felt deeply sorry that a relatively young man could have such a nervous disorder -- or possibly too much coffee already? Herbert began to doze then suddenly, there she was! "I'm looking for Mr Right," murmured Ondine-

Nelly in Herbert's head. "But I'm always ending up with Mr not-quite-right."

At this point his then-fiancée had sighed an extra-long and possibly even dramatic sigh. "I truly hope," she murmured, "that it will end up different with you, Herb."

After five years? thought Herbert. But he was, as almost always, silent.

After another longer sigh Ondine-Nelly said "You can stick your tongue in my ear, Herb. I mean it!"

Herbert gladly did as required and Ondine-Nelly began to breathe heavily until, about thirty seconds later, she said firmly, "That's enough, Herb," and "Are you Mr Right, Herb? Or are you Mr not-quite-right?"

Herbert, of course had gently protested that they had, after all, been engaged for five years but Ondine-Nelly squeezed his hand affectionately and whispered "Life is a gamble, Herb. But if it's in the cards and if you've got the right hand, the Queen of Hearts will smile on you. 'Specially if you're a man in uniform, 'specially if you're a soldier! Or a sailor," she added beguilingly. "Stick your tongue back in my ear, Herb, back where it belongs -- for now. Soldier on! Show me if you're Mr Right!"

Herbert had stuck his tongue right back into his then-fiancée's ear and she had gasped "I love taking chances!"

"Chances?" he had asked, and pulled his tongue right out. "What sort of chances?"

"Life is a gamble, Herb, or weren't you listening? But I wouldn't let just anyone stick their tongue in my ear."

"Even after five years, darling?"

"Even after a hundred years!"

"It certainly is a gamble after a hundred years," Herbert had said, attempting to humour her. But Ondine-Nelly did not smile. She told him she was going, on Saturday, to marry Mr Suggs whom she had met in the local Laundromat on Thursday. Though Mr Suggs, to her knowledge, had never worn a uniform.

"That slut is a weirdo," muttered Herbert's grandmother on Monday.

"I'm going to London on Tuesday, Ma," said Herbert, who always called his dear grandmother "Ma".

"Good for what ails you, honey," she had said.

Herbert woke suddenly and wiped a tear of remembrance from his eye.

"It's an elegant little flat, dear," Aubrey was saying as he gently prodded Herbert out of their taxi. "A bit of a march up some stairs but well worth it."

They climbed numerous pea-green carpeted stairs covered with orange flowers past acres of silver polka-dotted, black wallpaper. At last at Aubrey's door, they stood under a gigantic revolving chandelier made of a huge, inverted feet-in-the-air chromium beetle with holes in its back from which numerous tiny red spotlights rotated over the landing. "I personally chose this for my landlord. I dabble in interior design," said Aubrey.

The lamp's tiny red spotlights sweeping over his face, Herbert tilted dangerously for a better view of this unmissable chandelier. He was too far gone to be critical even if he'd known how. "It's a beaut!" he managed,

"So are you, love," whispered Aubrey, also red-illumined and totally devoted.

"I'm glad you suggested this," said Herbert, swaying gently against a wall as Aubrey unlocked the glossy black-painted door to his tiny flat, "It's been tough going lately trying to forget Ondine-Nelly."

"*Who's* nelly?" said Aubrey, with the very slightest of frowns.

"My Nelly," said Herbert. "It's been pretty tough lately trying to forget that lovely little vixen. A nice hot cup of coffee will perk me up just fine."

"I do truly hope so," whispered Aubrey who leered

pleasantly, opened his door and nudged Herbert through it.

Herbert abruptly stopped swaying, braced himself against a wall and began to sob as he happily scanned the small room before him. "Oh God! Ondine-Nelly would have loved this place! She adored black walls and black plastic bedspreads and black, acrylic fake-fur rugs!"

Herbert, sobbing unashamedly, dropped himself on the black plastic covered sofa-bed as it was the only place to sit in this tiny room other than a very high, black enameled stool that stood hard by what might have been a tiny, fold-out dining table. Herbert closed his eyes and hunched drunkenly as his ex-fiancée lurched once again into his head. "Black is the colour of my true love's hair," breathed Ondine-Nelly, in better days, softly into Herbert's ear.

"But my hair is red, darling," protested Herbert.

"You're a stickler for details, aren't you Herb? I'm not sure I like that."

The next day Ondine-Nelly had gone to the Laundromat with her black towels and black tablecloths and one large black bathroom mat and met uniform-less Mr Suggs.

"Lay down, dear," said Aubrey motioning with a large black plastic covered pillow, "and I'll tuck this right behind your head and make you comfy whilst I set the coffee water on to hot-up. Take off your trousers if you like."

Aubrey tucked the black plastic pillow tenderly behind Herbert's head.

"Take off my trousers?" managed Herbert still dangling in the dregs of his daydream.

"It'll make you more comfy," said Aubrey smiling pleasantly from a tiny wall basin as he filled an electric kettle.

"I suppose I would be more comfortable without my trousers," mumbled Herbert into his chest, "These wool trousers do scratch."

Herbert didn't hear the tiny gasp of pleasure emitted by Aubrey from his basin as he filled his electric kettle. "Goody!"

cried Aubrey and set down the kettle and switched it on.

Herbert wondered why Aubrey had found it good that his wool trousers had scratched but assumed, as he clumsily struggled them off that he had misunderstood him.

"My, my, *my!*" exclaimed Aubrey from his tiny basin, "White cotton Y-fronts! How shall I put this? You do fill them well!"

"Thank you," slurred Herbert whose eighth double scotch had more than begun to click in. He thought how considerate Aubrey was in his, Herbert's, hour of need. But he could not, absolutely could not get Ondine-Nelly out of his head. It was simply habit, he told himself. Five years of virulent habit. His recollections of his ex-fiancée were built layer upon layer like the remains of an ancient city. Like the ruins of Troy. Herbert smiled with pride over this delightful and, rare for him, turn of phrase then lapsed happily into a kind of archaeological lethargy.

"I am going to put something very special in your coffee," whispered Aubrey. "The boy upstairs is a medical student and provides me with a ready supply of ethylated spirits. That is, pure alcohol. It will relax you."

Aubrey poured a liberal amount of something from a small purple bottle into a shiny black cup of steaming water, added several teaspoonfuls of powdered coffee and handed it to Herbert, who bent sleepily up from his huge black plastic pillow.

"Excuse me whilst I freshen up and slip into something more comfy," said Aubrey and disappeared behind a black velvet curtain he had pulled to conceal a small area around the water basin. To Herbert's knowledge a proper bathroom did not exist.

Herbert, now temporarily abandoned by the phantom of his former fiancée, lazily sipped his pure-alcohol-laced coffee and felt warmer and more welcome than at any time since his arrival in icy England early the day before -- it was now well after midnight. He was grateful to Aubrey for this warming potion and the four, just noticed, electric heaters placed strategically round the shiny, black plastic quilted sofa-bed and the surprisingly comfy black plastic pillow propped behind his head. He began to doze and drifted into a fantasy he often day-dreamt when "the world was too much with him" and he felt himself lifted joyously heavenward, guffawing happily in the arms of some deeply humorous person of indeterminate gender. Then suddenly there was Ondine-Nelly, chanting one of her numerous, educative poems!

> "When you can laugh
> While those around you cry
> When you can smile
> While others sigh
> And tear their hair
> When you can say:
> I have got other fish to fry
> Then you're a man, my son
> And you've got balls to spare!
> When you --"

Herbert heard fussy little noises coming from behind the black velvet curtain where Aubrey had retired to freshen up and slip into something more comfortable. Herbert heard the water faucet turned off and on several times, the clinking of small glass bottles and the intrusive sound of an electric hair dryer. As he listened to this symphony of wee-hour ablutions he stared down at his legs which stretched striklingly in front of him on the shiny black plastic bedspread. He followed his sturdy legs back to his plump, according to Aubrey, fully adequate crotch. But if his sturdy legs or "well-filled" crotch were ever an advantage for Herbert with "the ladies" he had yet to discover it. He followed his legs again down to his toes and began to feel downright peculiar. "My head is beginning to swim. I seem to be having delusions of grandeur," he mumbled as this tiny room spun and suddenly become the interior of a spacious and richly appointed boudoir from Ondine-Nelly's picture volume: 'Everybody's Famous Boudoirs'.

"I could get real sexed up on a bed like that!" cried Herbert's ex-fiancée. "Doesn't it get you all hot and bothered, Herb?"

"Indeed it does, darling," said Herbert. "No doubt about that."

"So whaddaya gonna do about it, Herb?"

"Let me embrace you, dear," said Herbert.

"Christ! I wouldn't take a pee in this dump!" said Ondine-Nelly as the richly appointed boudoir of his imagination suddenly became Herbert's own modest rental. "When are ya gonna get a decent apartment, Herb?! I need a little luxury around me so's I can let down my hair! So's I can really let go! I can be a lotta fun when you get to know me!"

"My darling, I have known you for five years and I have never known you to be boring or inattentive," said Herbert tenderly.

"Jee-sus!" said Ondine-Nelly, "I'm late for choir practice! Get the lead out and get me to the church on time, Herb!"

The ethylated spirits began now to work wonders in Herbert's jet-fatigued head as Ondine-Nelly's betrayal and defection to Mr Suggs suddenly grew fainter.

Aubrey's room now returned in all its ebony glory as Aubrey, crying "Voila!" sprang naked through the abruptly parted black velvet curtain and landed, fully erect on the black plastic bedspread beside Herbert.

"He is taut with excitement" mumbled Herbert sleepily. Perhaps he is overtired. I have had that experience myself in my callow youth, mused Herbert, and began again to doze, too tired to further rationalize Aubrey's extreme rigidity.

"How shall I put it? What do you like to do?" breathed Aubrey heavily into Herbert's ear much in the manner of Ondine-Nelly. But Herbert was asleep.

"I said!" whispered Aubrey, much louder, also in the manner of Herbert's ex, "What do you like to do, Herbert?!"

One of Herbert's eyes limped open. "Do? What do I like to do?" Herbert had just, only seconds before, again stuck his tongue into Ondine-Nelly's ear and was about to hug and kiss her.

"Yes," whispered Aubrey, "What do you like to do?!

"I err... like to...swim..." Herbert dozed a bit, woke, "And sometimes I go out...for a drink...like tonight." He began again to doze.

"No, I mean sex-wise!" whispered Aubrey emphatically into Herbert's other ear and began to stroke Herbert's leg.

"Knee-pits," mumbled Herbert.

"Knee-pits?" repeated Aubrey breathily.

"The soft, downy back of the leg just behind...the knee," mumbled Herbert, abruptly losing consciousness.

"Here?" whispered Aubrey breathing faster as he brought his hand up the back of Herbert's closest knee.

Ondine-Nelly frowned in Herbert's head. "I find you extremely kinky, Herb. The knee-pit is not, by a long shot, considered an erogenous zone. Kindly confine your future erotic attentions to more normal channels. Like, for instance, the vagina." She frowned again. "I mean, of course, after we are wed. Until then, we can but discuss it at length."

"Let me caress you, Ondine-Nelly," Herbert had said.

"Herbert! Do you or don't you adore my new scent?!" cried Aubrey, attempting to shake Herbert awake. "It's called 'Black Funk'. I feel super-sensory in it. It comes in a holiday gift packet with a frank magazine and a tube of scented lubricant called 'Nature's Handmaiden'. Wake up and we'll peruse the magazine together. Let's face it. It's really very exciting!"

But Herbert dozed on, his eyes moving erratically under closed lids as he pursued his elusive ex-fiancée. After a moment, one of his eyes sluggishly opened then closed, and he whispered aloud "It's a funny old world."

"Indeed it is," mused Aubrey. "So we'd best get down to business."

Aubrey meticulously removed Herbert's tweedy jacket and tie and beautifully pressed white shirt and white t-shirt and tantalizing white underpants. He said "My, my, *my*!" as he surveyed the naked -- save his socks -- shapeliness of his snoozing new acquaintance. "Let's have you roll over on your tummy, dear. You'll be ever so much more comfy that way," whispered Aubrey. With some difficulty, he arranged Herbert on his stomach and moaned lustily.

Somewhere deep in his ethylated head Herbert was pleased with Aubrey's gentle courtesy and the fervour of his concern for his, Herbert's, comfort and he hoped that the whole British nation was as genuinely kind and unselfish and as pleasantly disposed as his new friend. "No more wars, no more wars," mumbled Herbert, and began to snore.

Lovingly, because he had so quickly developed an all embracing affection for him, Aubrey slipped off Herbert's socks, pulled Herbert's legs apart and carefully set a very large, black plastic cushion between them so they would remain so. "Sex-wise," Aubrey was whispering, "Sex-wise I prefer to leap like an agile gazelle upon the object of my affections." He then rose and placed the high, black enameled stool about two feet from the black plastic quilted sofa-bed where snoring Herbert lay, irresistibly naked, legs apart, upon his stomach.

Aubrey climbed up the tall stool and stood on its top, his bare, hairless legs wobbling only slightly as he again gazed reverently, rigidly, from a height, over Herbert's slim waist, firm smooth buttocks and sturdy, propped apart, legs.

"I leap!" shouted Aubrey, and would have, had not the tall, black enameled stool rocketed out from beneath him.

"We reap what we sow!" cried Ondine-Nelly in Herbert's head. "I just might go all-the-way with you this evening, Herb. As a gesture of good faith in hopes that you will one day be rich or in uniform or both."

Four days later Ondine-Nelly became Mrs Ondine-Nelly Suggs.

"That slut's a weirdo!" grumbled Herbert's grandmother.

"Herbert?"

"Ondine-Nelly?!" cried Herbert.

"Herbert?" whispered Aubrey. "Herbert, my dear, please wake up."

"Ondine-Nelly!?" cried Herbert, and abruptly sat up.

"Herbert," whispered Aubrey, prostrate on his black acrylic-fur carpeted floor, "Listen carefully. You must go down the stairs to the third landing immediately. There you will find a telephone. You must call an ambulance. How shall I put it? I seem to have broken my leg."

BIG GERTRUDE

"Sybil, tired of conquest, weary of sub-
mission, slumped sleepily against a tree
in the high summer sunshine of London's Hyde Park gazing with sublime
satisfaction at her own gorgeous legs."

Gertrude stopped typing, grinned and took a sip of black
coffee, carefully set the cup back in its saucer and typed:

"Suddenly Sybil became aware of a figure
beside her. Not surprisingly, considering
her scanty attire and her ultra-gorgeous
legs, it was the figure of an extraordinarily
handsome young man, dark-haired and
clad in exceedingly tight, fashionably tattered blue-jeans, the sumptuous, bulging
crotch of which, shamelessly celebrated
his glorious, rising maleness!"

Gertrude stopped again, grinned again, and typed:

"Sybil's sharp, mercilessly made-up eyes
gaped in sweet wonder at this fetching
young male lying on the grass not an
arm's length away. Despite her fatigue she
began to float helplessly, like white froth
on a soon-to-break wave. She was pow-
erless, a slave to something much larger,

she did fervently hope, than herself."

Annie, who had lived in the flat above Gertrude, loved to laugh with Gertrude over an evening coffee. Especially after their creation of the fabulous, fictional Sybil, patterned comically after Annie herself. Annie, who had taught painting, could be as silly as Gertrude was overly serious. Annie, in her way, taught Gertrude to lighten up, to laugh more. Now that Annie wasn't here anymore the task fell to Sybil, their spiritual child, as Annie used to call her. Gertrude took a sip of coffee, thought of Annie, thought of Sybil, and typed:

> "With a resounding rip this beddable young man's zipper was torn asunder and thrust skyward was the sleekest, shapeliest--"

On the desk at Gertrude's elbow, an ancient alarm clock went off. Startled, she slammed it silent, muttered "Damn!" grabbed a light summer jacket from a hook by the door and stormed out of her tiny apartment to the bus stop.

"Fares! Fares, please!" called the conductor striding cheerfully down the bus aisle.

"Sorry," said Gertrude dropping into her favourite window seat, "I've only got a fiver."

"That's all right, love," said the conductor, a friendly and attractive middle aged woman, as the bus started off with a grinding lurch. "I hope you don't mind small change, duckie," she said, counting it over another passenger's head into Gertrude's palm.

"Fares! Fares, please!" she called and continued, smiling, down the aisle, clicking out tickets from the impeccably polished chromium machine around her neck. She reminded Gertrude of her dearest Annie, minus, of course, the ticket machine. The bus conductor was about the age Annie would have been. So much, too much, reminded Gertrude of Annie. Especially lately.

This daily bus journey always made Gertrude sleepy. So she usually closed her eyes and fixed them on imaginary blank pages and filled these pages with words that would become silly stories which, to her amazement, she had recently begun to sell to several pulp magazines. Half-dozing, and immersed in the dull roar of traffic she perused these pages in her newly minted, paid-author's mind:

> "Sybil, the cheerful bus conductor, when there were bus conductors on those wonderful, red, door-less buses, was fifty-two and unusually well-preserved for her age. Her firm middle-aged legs glowed white hot beneath the seeming innocence of her crisp, well-ironed London Transport uniform. Her sleek, shimmering skin was attractive to men, indeed, irresistible to men. But she had held herself back for years, not daring to loose the lust that lurked at the libidinous core of her being -- the seething passion that she knew, full well, could and would, destroy her lock, stock and barrel!"

The bus lurched to a stop. "Mind your step, please!" called the cheerful conductor. "Mind your step!"

The bus started up. "Hold tight, please! Hold tight!"

Gertrude's eyes had blinked open but soon closed and she continued her story:

> "Then it happened! He was a good three decades younger than the perfectly pre-

served Sybil and the only fare on the bus!
A dart of her mercilessly mascaraed eyes
instantly told her that the fetching young
man was also hyperbolically hung -- and
that did it!

'I've had enough of holding myself
back!' hissed Sybil through gleaming
teeth that were her own. This much
younger man leered lasciviously from
beneath his shining sheath of sleek black
hair as he became instantly aware of
Sybil's fine, shimmering skin. Needless
to say, he had already sensed the palpable
heat from her unusually firm, hot, simply
gorgeous middle-aged legs! Sybil smoul-
dered a meaningful smile and in a trice
he was upon her! 'CRIKEY!' he shouted,
pushing aside her impeccably polished
ticket machine, 'I never thought it could
be like this!' "

'I'm ever so glad I didn't hold myself
back,' sighed Sybil, with a pleasant smile
only minutes later, as she pulled on her
crisp, well ironed London Transport
uniform and hung the impeccably polished ticket machine around her neck
where it belonged."

"Isn't this your stop, love?" inquired the friendly conductor.
Gertrude, startled from her daydream story, thanked this
ever-helpful woman, climbed off the bus and started slowly
up the steps to the school where she taught an Art Therapy
class. Annie had recommended Gertrude, who had an art
degree, for the job when she, Annie, was no longer able.

"Its excellent, Tom. Your best work yet. I love your bold

colour. You're handling paint very well now."

The fifteen year old, freckled boy was ecstatic. "It's you, Miss! But not so big as you was before."

"Oh, it looks just like me." said Gertrude, "Only not as big as I was before."

Gertrude was pleased. Tom was her best student and she could honestly say that the painting was an excellent likeness and artfully done -- though it seemed so much thinner and far more fragile than she had imagined herself. She had always thought of herself as big. Big Gertrude. Now she could be ordinary Gertrude. Everyday Gertrude.

"I love you, Miss."

"I love you too, Tom."

"Will you love me always?"

"As long as I can. Promise. Excuse me, Tom, Ethel seems to be eating her watercolours. I'll be back in a minute, love."

Gertrude moved easily to a large elderly woman and gently as possible removed a watercolour box from the woman's stubborn grip.

"Pardon me, Ethel, shouldn't you save your colours for that lovely flower you've just painted? I think flowers are your favourites aren't they?"

"How did you know?!"

"Because you paint them so beautifully. Flowers are my favourites too."

"Are they?"

"Absolutely! Here comes the tea lady."

"Goody!" cried Ethel.

The short dark woman in black at the tea trolley handed Gertrude a cup of tea.

"I never have milk, Mrs Vespucci. Only lemon," said Gertrude.

"Fussy, are we, Miss Queen of Sheba?" snarled Vespucci.

"You know I always have lemon," said Gertrude, attempting to be reasonable with this woman who'd been unceasingly rude since Gertrude began teaching this class two years before, just after...

"Then I'll 'ave the tea back, if you please!"

Vespucci grabbed the cup from Gertrude but it toppled from her hand and splashed over Ethel's painting."

"You've ruined her painting!" cried Gertrude.

"She won't take no notice. They're all mental here, Miss Queen of Sheba, or didn't you know? I'll just tidy it up for her."

Gertrude could take no more, drew herself up and pushed the woman away. "Get away from her, you destructive woman! Get away!"

Gertrude was cautioned by the headmistress that afternoon but she didn't give a damn. Her contract was almost up and she had already decided not to renew it.

Before catching her bus home she remembered she needed a loaf of bread and started down the street to a small shop. After a moment she was aware she was being followed by Mrs Vespucci and a frowning cohort. Gertrude was unafraid, turned and faced them squarely, pugnaciously, and hurried on, leaving puzzled Vespucci and her frowning woman friend far behind as she wrote a new page in her head:

> "Vespucci had the mad, yellow eyes of a vulture and she dressed always in black and used black lipstick and painted her nails black. The colour of death suited her. For there were men who lusted after that sort of thing and this evening was rife with them. Five such, stood waiting, panting and shivering lascivi- ously, drowning in their own concupis- cence at the bar in the local pub Vespucci frequented. One never knew who the churlish, black clad woman would choose. As these five prospective victims

stood waiting they became ever hotter with anticipation, their Latin lusts rising clumsily, even visibly, against their worn, shiny black trousers. An evening with Vespucci, the Portuguese tea-lady, was legendary but could be perilous. Some-times one never came back."

"For God's sake!" shouted the driver as he braked his car, narrowly avoiding Gertrude. "Open your eyes, woman! You'll kill yourself!"

"Sorry, love!" called Gertrude, not as startled as she might have been, "I'd thought of it!"

That night Gertrude went to sleep mid-sentence over her keyboard. She was unusually tired.

"Hold tight, please. Fares please! Fares!" Gertrude was in her favourite window seat and already drowsing as her bus, in fits and starts, valiantly battled peak hour London.

"You give 'em back!" shouted a boy at the rear of the bus.

"Won't!" shouted a second boy.

"You will!" shouted the first boy.

"Won't! Make me!"

The same, good-natured conductor said "Give him back his sweets, love. I saw you take 'em."

"I won't!" shouted the second boy.

"You will or you'll be put off this public conveyance!"

"Give 'em back!" cried the first boy, near tears.

"No!" insisted the other boy, and, turning to the kind conductor, cried "You better be careful how you talk to me! My Dad's in the Mob!"

"Sybil awakened slowly. Her London Transport uniform was severely rumpled exposing her smooth but firm, hot legs. Her lacy, black knickers lay crumpled around her sleek ankles,"

wrote Gertrude in her head -- Annie would have loved it!

> "All Sybil could remember was the defiant
> boy's last blatant wink as he offered her
> a handful of his own colourful sweets
> to avoid being put off her bus. Why, oh
> why had she accepted those drugged
> jelly-beans, eaten so many of them? This
> Mobster's child looked harmless enough
> but --"

"Western Hospital!" cried the conductor. Gertrude bolted upright in her seat.

"Isn't this your stop, love?" smiled the pleasant conductor.

"Yes thanks," cried Gertrude who hopped off just before the bus, at the conductor's bell, started away. The kind woman's "Mind your step, love," sang comfortingly in Gertrude's head and she thought of Annie as she made her way up the hospital steps.

"Hello, Gertrude," said the nurse as Gertrude entered.

"Hello."

"Right on time dear. But we're behind schedule today. I'm afraid there'll be a wait."

Gertrude nodded and sat. She was the only one in the waiting room. Her treatment appointments were usually late afternoon as her teaching schedule made earlier times difficult. Fortunately the hospital lay on the same bus route as her Art Therapy class. And the friendly bus ticket-taker was a treasure.

"There are new magazines on the table, love. One you might like. We're subscribing to a car magazine now, too, for the men. And you, of course." The nurse blushed becomingly. "Men seem to like car magazines like you do. I remembered."

"How thoughtful," smiled Gertrude who had never met an automobile she didn't love. "You are kind," said Gertrude with another smile as the nurse disappeared.

After about forty minutes the nurse reappeared and said the doctor was going over Gertrude's treatment history with a fine-tooth comb. The doctor would see her in ten minutes for a long consultation. Tomorrow was the big day, wasn't it? Time to test if her grueling series of treatments had been successful. Certainly, they'd helped her shed unwelcome weight, hadn't they?

The nurse disappeared again and Gertrude, happily thumbing through the latest edition of her favourite car magazine, hummed a jolly little ditty Annie had taught her several years before. She knew all the verses and surprised herself. She missed her Annie. Ten minutes passed. Then twenty. She began to hum the little ditty again but found that this time, after she'd got through the second verse, she couldn't remember the others at all. None of them. So she sighed and gave up.

It was crushingly warm. Annie should have been here. She'd have made some withering joke about the nurse's hair or the woman in a bikini on the cover of the car magazine. Or the horrible heat. It was far too warm today, unbearable! Gertrude thumbed through a few more pages of the car magazine. Annie would certainly have said something to make her smile. Gertrude sighed, put down the magazine, went to a window and opened it as wide as it would open. She stood there a moment peering through the hot, shimmering air that rose like steam from a small strip of decorous garden. Gertrude sighed again and whispered:

> "Tomorrow she'll be tested.
> They'll say it's been arrested.
> And who is she to quibble?
> So it appeared to Sybil."

ISLAND QUEEN

They hummed and murmured amongst her jumble of objets d'art and the elegant furnishings of her 99th floor penthouse apartment. The subtly audible noises seemed to come from nowhere and everywhere and they unnerved her. She'd had every expert in town up to investigate. Her problem was insoluble. No one could hear the odd noises. No one but her.

The noises had begun exactly one month before. The day she had posted to her son and daughter each a tiny jewel-encrusted cell phone, an exact replica of her own. Upon returning home that day she had announced to her neatly coiffed image in a Louis XIV mirror that these gifts would either encourage her errant, overgrown tots to communicate with their generous Mommy, or purse-strings-holding Mommy would know the reason why. The noises had begun just then, precisely then, immediately after her rueful announcement to that old French mirror. Immediately after she had uttered the words *the reason why*.

Damn it! She had spent a fortune on her ungrateful kids for nearly two decades. But she had a fortune to spend -- several, in fact. Plus a bit more. Possibly even more than that.

She sprawled in her white leather chair and sipped regularly from an enormous goblet of ancient brandy. There, amidst the disquieting ebb and flow of these unnerving noises, she gazed down at the city far below, a healthy chunk of which, after her recent fabulous divorce settlement, now belonged to her. But if she were queen of Manhattan Island, as many insisted, why couldn't this odd noise problem be solved? What the hell were they anyhow, these wretched whispers, these hummings and murmurs and mumblings, these soft almost-but-not-quite-voices that seemed to be trying to tell her something?!

She snatched a cigarette from a gold case, stuffed it carelessly into her ivory cigarette holder -- she'd commandeered this stunning holder from the hand of an unfortunate shopper at the priciest antique shop in town. She lit her cigarette with a gold lighter in the shape of a tiny caryatid from some Greek temple -- she couldn't care less which. What she didn't know about Greek temples, she'd say with a grin, would fill the Parthenon. And that Greek gentleman who'd given the lighter... She smiled. One day, she had promised herself, she would actually read a book about objets d'art as her divorce settlement had provided a ton of 'em.

She inhaled, exhaled dramatically through her nose, sipped her ancient brandy and tried vainly to relax in her superbly tailored black raw-silk, red satin-lined pants-suit. She nervously dipped a multi-ringed finger into her brandy, ran it round the rim of the goblet till the glass hummed and resonated crazily with the odd, whispery noises that had continued unnervingly apace.

She listened and fretted for another moment, kneaded her superbly pedicured toes into fine, white carpet, and tried to concentrate on relaxing. It was futile.

"This ain't helping one damned bit!" she announced and grabbed her tiny jeweled telephone from a silken pocket and punched a number.

"It's me, Richard, your gorgeous ex-wife... I know I shouldn't be ringing you again... I know I rang you an hour ago... but... Please, Richard! It's not about my party. I know you aren't coming. It's those goofy noises! They're driving me insane!... What, Richard?!"

She clipped her tiny, jewel-encrusted telephone near an emerald broach on the lapel of her raw-silk suit and poured another brandy.

"Oh yes, Richard! It's the trees!" she cried amenably -- their twelfth-century, Russian Icon -- or whatever the hell it was, was still in dispute and amenable was her word for the day... "Ahhh Nature!" she cooed amenably into her tiny telephone, "Oh Richard, I am so relieved!"

She wasn't at all relieved and exclaimed after she'd beeped him off, "Trees on the ninety-ninth floor? My terrace isn't even planted yet!"

She swigged at her brandy, sighed, "One hour ago he said it was the sound of the sea! Anyhow, he bores me up the wall!"

She dialed her telephone, grinned, waited, shouted "Richard, you bore me up the wall!" She giggled as she beeped off the tiny mobile. Phooey to that Russian icon -- or whatever it is! Who needs twelfth-century icons?! This was more fun! She found she had forgotten the unnerving noises for a moment and laughed gratefully and quaffed her ancient brandy. She poured another and took a hefty swig and peered down through her colossal glass wall double-checking that her personal portion of the city so far below was still there. Glory! It was! She sighed with the singular pleasure of outrageous ownership and giggled: "I am sick and tired of Richard and I don't care who knows it."

She re-lit her failing cigarette with the gold caryatid lighter, puffed it to life, inhaled and exhaled elaborately as she peered at her reflection in the massive glass wall and shuddered at a subtle increase in volume of her strange noises.

She rose and marched through ankle-deep carpet to a tall, black lacquered Chinese cabinet -- screw which dynasty -- took out a white-tiger-skin covered box and obtained from it a tiny bottle of scarlet nail polish. She returned to her white leather sofa, and her cigarette and her goblet of ancient brandy and snatched up her tiny telephone and punched a number. Sighing, she again clipped the tiny apparatus by her emerald broach and began to paint her nails and muttered "I'm sick and tired of Richard and I don't care who knows it... Hello, Jane, darling? I'm sick and tired of Richard and I don't care who knows it... what's up, honey? Coming to my little party?... Oh, poop! I was counting on you... No, no, Richard will as usual not be here. That's why I divorced him, ain't it?! He paid for my parties but he never came! Anyhow, he bores me up the wall... No, honey, no real news on that front either... dammit! I wasn't going to mention it! I feel sorta, kinda down in the dumps about it... Well, if you must know, this morning Tommy returned my nifty little birthday present air express from Istanbul. No letter, no note, no nothin'. Just that tiny, jewel-encrusted, smart-phone. What the hell is Tommy doing in Istanbul?!... I didn't even know he was in Istanbul!... Janie! Did you hear that?!... Hold on, Janie!"

She carefully laid her nail brush in a cut-crystal ashtray quaffed the last of her goblet, added more, and with goblet in hand, waded through lush carpet to the far side of the palatial living room. She cocked her ear to the odd noises which seemed now to swell from her spectacular cinema/ entertainment room opposite, stood there a moment listening, shook her head, sipped, returned and sat. "Did you hear that, honey? Noises?... You didn't?... Janie, you must be half deaf!... sorry, dear, I'd forgotten. Well darling it's your own fault. You're always losing those itsy-bitsy batteries, aren't you?... Really, honey, they do fall out so terribly easily. And when they fall out they're so difficult to see, particularly in quality carpeting. I believe I squashed one of your little beasties under my golf spikes the last time you were here... ages ago?"

She took up her delicate nail brush, continued to paint. "... If you must know, Janie, I am deeply disappointed in you... not coming to my party yet again. You live only thirty floors below me and you never come to my parties. Why is that, honey?... Yes dear, I do know what serious illness can mean and you don't have to be so huffy about it -- God knows I've suffered too. Terribly... Well, you know how I despise dental visits.... Yeah, sure... uh-huh... But couldn't you just roll him to the elevator in that expensive contraption of his?... Well I do hope your ailing spouse gets well one day, for all our sakes. I could use a little company way the hell up here on top of the goddamned world... Goodbye, Jane!"

She winced and beeped off. The telephone rang and with a hopeful smile she beeped it on. "Janie, honey? I'm so sorry, dear. I didn't mean to be insensitive... Oh. Ms Brown! Why didn't you say it was you?" She frowned. "I've been meaning to call you about the sandwiches... Yes, Ms Brown, about tonight. My petite soirée... I do hope you've remembered. Last week I got only half the crab-salad sandwiches I ordered. I am a woman who must be prepared for any eventuality. Us dames get that way when we reach fifty... Yeah, honey, that's so right. It is at the age of fifty that all hell breaks loose... Tommy? Oh, he's fine, I guess... Yes, he is a big boy now."

She laughed. "Tommy said, the day he left, that he intended to flaunt his buff body in the major capitals of the world for favors and money... Tommy doesn't need money, Ms Brown. Favors I can understand. Every boy needs a little affection now and then -- from wherever, whenever, whoever -- and I myself was never one to turn down a solid gold cigarette lighter..." She snatched up the caryatid lighter, gazed dreamily at it, snapped it into fire, snapped it shut. "But money...God! There was always plenty of that around... Yes, Debbie is off flaunting somewhere too. Amsterdam, at the moment, I think. I am astonished to say that both of my children just up and disappeared from their last known address like a goddamned spray deodorant. I sent them each a spectacular custom-made cell phone -- a mobile, dear, you know, two jewel-encrusted copies of mine -- for their birthdays last month... They were born on the same day, a year apart. I have not heard word one from either of them for two years... just those little address-change-thingies, those dreary little discolored cards smelling of mold and derelict foreign post offices. Yuk! But Tommy and Debbie always make sure Mommy knows precisely where to send their next check! Addictive, ain't it? Money? Happily,

I've found that to be so... Incidentally, Ms Brown, it's my own birthday today too. I've told absolutely nobody. I refuse to make a big fuss of it. And I won't hold my breath for prezzies. I haven't had much luck with birf-days lately!"

From the corner of her superbly-mascaraed eye she could have sworn she'd just seen the figure of a young person moving about in her cinema/entertainment room opposite -- like in the old days. She set down her brandy, knew then she'd had the teeniest bit too much. It was the noises that caused her to rely on the brandy. She never, ever drank alone till now. Or did she? But could that dim figure in the next room be her beloved son? Or her beloved daughter? On a surprise birf-day visit?! Yes. She'd had more than one too many. It was those goddamned noises, wasn't it?

"Ms Brown? Are you still there, Ms Brown?... Good. Can you do me the honour of explaining why I have received, sandwich-wise, only half of what I expected?" Her voice was blurring more than a little. "Yes it is a funny old world and I deeply appreciate your apparent interest in philosophy but you are a capitalist, my dear, in your own way and we are dealing here with the humble sandwich. Your catering affair provides a crucial service for our considerable skyscraper community. Last week I received only half as many sandwiches as I expected... Yes, I know I always send back the leftovers for the help, but..."

The doorbell chimed a pleasant little melody as a small screen beside her chimed in unison and she saw a special delivery postman standing just outside her door with a small package. "Got to go, Ms Brown, mailman's here with a birf-day prezzie for me! Imagine that!"

'Birf-day' was what she'd called it in the nursery when the children were younger and things were so much easier. When the world seemed right and sensible. Not upside-down and full of crazy noises, like now... She'd not even had time to hire a new staff after Richard had fled with the cook, maid, and housekeeper. New staff were impossible to find without months of vetting ...or one could hire help who'd abscond with everything not bolted down! It was common on her island.

She beeped off, lurched to the door and returned unsteadily a moment later and dropped herself into the white leather chair and set the package on the table beside. She quaffed the goblet, poured another and struggled for a moment unwrapping the package then stopped, stared blankly at it and whispered "My birf-day gift to Debbie. She sent it back from Amsterdam. My birf-day gift to Tommy. He sent his back from Istanbul. No letters, no notes, no nothin'. What am I gonna do with two more goddamned cell phones?"

The odd noises built slightly in volume. Humming and mumbling, they subtly, now even pleasantly, floated through her magnificently air-conditioned evening.

"Richard says my goofy noises are the sound of the sea. Richard says that when you live on an island you're bound to hear the sound of the sea." She took up her goblet and sipped. "But I know better."

She was now certain that at least one of her children was moving about in the entertainment room opposite. Maybe preparing a surprise birthday party? Reassured, she grinned sleepily and thought that in a minute or two she would light another delightful, ivory-holdered cigarette with that splendid, gold caryatid lighter and she'd ring Ms Brown and order more sandwiches for tonight. The children, both of them, loved crab salad sandwiches too. She would order many more. Later, when she was rested, but before the party, she might begin a book about objets d'art -- what she didn't know about objets d'art could... "Never mind," she muttered reassuringly into her goblet and caught a glimpse of her perfectly cared-for face in her glass wall and grinned amiably, sleepily.

The odd, now comforting, noises lulled her. She dozed, still wondering why at least one of her children hadn't emerged from that immense room opposite to wish her happy birf-day.

SOME EXCEEDINGLY KIND LADIES

(excerpt from the novel, LEMON GULCH, 2000, 2010)

I look up at the sign over the door.

> THE JOLLY JUG
> Formerly The Maiden's Head

Plus underneath of this sign is another sign which says:

> There ain't no other place
> just like this place
> anywhere near this place.
> So this must be the place.

I gobble down the last one of my 3 Milky-Ways plus enter in and look around for The Lonely Gal. The jukebox which is red and orange sits in a exceptionally dark segment of this Quasi-dark big room plus plays:

> "You broke my heart
> And throwed its little pieces on the dirty,
> stinkin' floor..."

My yellow little teeth commences to chatter like they traditionally do while nerve racked plus this Quasi-dark big room is roasting! (Due to the external merciless sun Indubitably.)

On the right side of said room is a pool table and 2 beauteous ladies is rubbing blue chalk on to the tips of their pool sticks and drinking beer from cans. Neither of said is The Lonely Gal as neither of said is lonely as they got each other as Colleagues. Hence ain't.

On the left side of said room is a green shuffleboard with 6 skinny Chromized legs. A short-haired lady in a red baseball cap which also holds a can of beer has jist made a shot plus is leaning over said shuffleboard laughing with one of her 2 feet kicking up in the air. She ain't The Lonely Gal neither as said Gal don't never laugh as Loneliness ain't no Laughing Matter. (Sadly.)

A contiguous lady claps her hands and wipes her Prespiring face on to her sleeve plus takes a swallow from her can of beer which she grabs off from a table. This lady ain't The Lonely Gal neither as how can she be lonely if she possesses one laughing friend?

OH MY GOSH! If none of these indeterminant Individuals is The Lonely Gal then where is she?!

All of said 4 ladies is garbed in satin black shirts with "THE STEAMROLLERS" printed in red big print acrosst their respectable 4 backs. All of said 4 ladies wear black slacks plus all of said 4 oscillates their multiple heads and notes me. This ain't no big surprise as every fool plus their brother always notes me in Incomprehensible Ways whenever I am On The Scene so to speak.

"Yeah?" says the short-haired lady in the red baseball cap which leans on this green skinny legged shuffleboard, "What can we do you for?"

"I'm l-looking for The L-Lonely G-Gal," I utter as Courteous as feasible.

"Get the kid a coke, Lorraine," says said lady to her Colleague at said shuffleboard, "He's gonna need it!"

"Sure, Babe," says Lorraine, "The poor kid is burnin' up! See how red he is?"

"Th-Thank you for your c-concern," I utter plus hope I ain't about to Fervantly keel over, "b-but I am always r-reddish

like thus p-plus I ain't got enough m-money to p-purchase no
c-coke."

This ain't explicitly a Truism as I got a Modicum of funds
but said is preserved for purchasing additional Milky-Ways
for dinner as I am getting hungry already.

Said lady smiles. "It's on me, kid. I'm Babe".

"Th-Then I w-would p-prefer a D-Dr P-Pepper, ma'am." (As
Dr Peppers is my all time favorite beverage even although
Coke is The Favorite Of Millions The World Over.) (I adore Ice
cold milk also.) (Whenever Applicable.)

"Get the kid a Dr P, Lorraine," says Babe which takes a
red bandana out from her hip pocket plus wipes it back and
fourth on to her Prespiring brows.

"Th-Thank you v-very much, Miss B-Babe." I utter grateful.

"Don't think nothin' of it, kiddo, but can the "Miss" stuff.
I'm jist plain Babe."

Babe smiles and Dislodges away my bitter reminiscences
of the unkind Receptionist which was fresh among my brains
as unkind items habitually loiter where No Loitering is
preferred.

As I await for my Dr Pepper I oscillate my head and peer
Eagerly in variegated directions in this dark big room and
can now jist make out the head of a Somnolent lady which is
laying with same (The head.) on a table contiguous by the bar.
My brains zoom! Is this The Lonely Gal?! The jukebox plays :

> "On the night I was born
> My pore daddy was torn
> With a sorrow as great as could be..."

This must be The Lonely Gal as even although Somnolent
she looks as lonely as all heck.

> "...I was the apple of Dad's eye
> But I caused him to cry

'Cause the Good Lord took Mama, you
see..." (Plays said jukebox.)

I ponder if The Lonely Gal lost her mother or father or some Individual Dear and Near with her. When persons asks about my Dad Bull I always say that Bull is croaked instead of a Thwarted Inebriant as I do not desire to answer Probing Questions as Prolongated Chat on my one legged Dad Bull traditionally impels me to blubber. Please do not ask me why. As I can not tell you. As I do not know.

Lorraine brings me my Dr Pepper spilled over 3 ice cubes. I thank her Courteous and take one behemoth swallow and consume nearly all of said then point one finger and suddenly say:

"Ain't th-that The L-Lonely G-Gal over th-there?"

"The one and only, hon," says Lorraine, "In all her glory. She is resting up for her broadcast tonight and there she is."

"Sleepin' it off," says Babe which notes Lorraine with Infinite kindness.

"Always sleepin' it off," says Lorraine. "Poor thing."

I ain't able to yank my piglet 2 eyes off from that Somnolent lady. "I g-got a m-m...m-m...m-message..."

"Set down before you fall down, honey," says Babe.

I feel excessively woozy so I set down on a high stool with a hot leatherette plastic red seat and although my heinie commences to itch Rapaciously I utter repetitiously:

"I g-got a m-message for h-her."

I am currently woozier even plus hope I do not keel over before I can utter what I have came to utter.

"She'll wake up in a minute, kiddo," says Babe. "What's your name?"

"D-Danny."

"You in love with her too, Danny Boy?" says Lorraine.

"Everybody's in love with The Lonely Gal, Danny," says Babe, "But she don't love nobody. Not since..."

Lorraine shakes her head at Babe which terminates her

prior sentence instantaneously.

"N-Not since w-what?" I say.

We hear glass smashing and oscillate our multiple heads. It is The Lonely Gal which has half-raised her head up from her table and shoved a empty beer mug off from it. She looks at I and the 4 additional ladies and hollers:

"What the fuck are you five fuckers gawking at?!"

"Ain't nobody here but us chickens," says Babe.

"Oh?!" says The Lonely Gal, "Oh!? Is that fucking so?!"

The Lonely Gal's head flops sideways plus says:

"How I loathe the contact of your fucking hostile eyes!"

Said head whacks right down on to the table then arises right up again like she is going to utter some additional item. But don't. Then said head whacks down plus comes up then whacks down again. I hope she ain't hurt herself! If I was not so woozy I would of waddled right up to her sleeping sides and patted her on her head genteel.

The 2 ladies at the pool table terminate their playing and Glare at her. I Ruminate that The Lonely Gal is all wrung out from sincere longing which is why she must of spoke fowl language as Jarleen sporadically Chats in these fowl Modes but don't mean nothing vital by it unless she is conversing with Bull and then she is fowl on purpose.

Anyhow. The Lonely Gal requires her strength as she has got her broadcast show tonight plus will benefit from a additional Cat-Nap as it is so darn hot and Enervating. (Said hotness nor Enervation can not never be Over Emphasized.) (As Southern California is severely Situated in a Sub-Tropical Climactic Belt.)

I myself am sweating like a stuck pig plus better not move from my leatherette red stool as I might weaken and flop to the floor. (Weight is heavy!)

However. I can not yank my piglet eyes off from said Gal plus am delightful that she ain't deformed nor Transfigured in no way whatsoever nor obese in the extremes like I myself which often impels brutal loneliness which I would not wish on no living Individual even me. (Nor don't!)

However. The Lonely Gal seems to be a Inebriant.

A concerned short lady comes out from a back room and commences to sweep up said Gal's broke beer mug which is scattered wide and far.

However. I know exactly what said Gal Inferred to when she uttered Hostile Eyes prior as a whole Bevy of said eyes Glares at me every day and I Loathe them. They follow me everywheres I go. I noted said Eyes on the horn-rim lady Receptionist and on that fatter even then I boy on the bus and Last But Not Least on the Inexorable PK Benderson. Eternally if not Incessantly!

So my heart fills right up for The Lonely Gal as I note her head laying there on that table in the Quasi-darkness adjacent besides of the bar. And I ponder The Multitudes of kind items which she utters habitually to me from my battery radio while the Jukebox plays:

> "Operator,
> Please connect me to Paradise
> I want to speak to Grandma
> Again..."

I pretend that I myself am a Orphan like them adapted 2 brothers in the Motion Picture and am watched over by The Lonely Gal which at this very minute commences to snore. I suddenly feel so heightened up that I holler:

"I L-LOVE TH-THAT L-LONELY G-GAL! I L-LOVE TH-THAT L-LONELY G-GAL!"

I must be a Madman to holler like this as all 4 said ladies abruptly oscillates and notes me With Alacrity!

Then everything gets woozy and I feel like I will either pee or keel over. I do both of those Simultaneous. When I awaken up the jukebox is playing:

"She was only a cowgirl in love..."

The room wobbles all over for one full interval then Little By Little I note all items more easy (Variegated objects like light bulbs and Ect. Ect. Ect.)

"...But her love was as big
as that big sky above..."

I am laying flat on my back pronely on the pool table with one pair of smelling bowling shoes underneath of my head for a pillow. Babe is fanning me with her red baseball cap and Lorraine is noting me with Overpowering Conjectures. I feel a Dire wetness on my Lower Pelvic Torsal Regions. AM I ABASHED!

"He has went and peed hisself, that poor fat kid," says one of the 2 ladies which has been playing pool. She squats down with her pool stick right besides of her pool table Compatriot which squats down similar approximately one foot behind of Babe.

"But it could of been worse, Reggie," says this squatting lady, "He could of pooped hisself."

Reggie kindly laughs. "We better get him offa this table, Marie, 'fore he wets it. Or somethin' even worse!"

Said 2 ladies desires to remove me off from the pool table top but Babe keeps fanning me and won't let them come contiguous plus utters:

"Let the poor kid cool off for a minute, gals, he's all fagged out."

"Well if you say so, Babe," says Reggie which Infers to my Heat Prostation. I myself am not excessively worried as I keel over a whole alots plus am Fully Accustomized. (As said.)

Lorraine brings me a additional Dr P spilled over 3 ice cubes plus says:

"On the house!"

Now ain't that a kind thing which to do? I set up and she smiles at me and hands me the Dr P. I am now brimming over with gratuities plus am totally conscionable.

I thank Lorraine then complement all 4 of these exceedingly kind ladies on their Gorgeous black shirts with "The Steamrollers" in red acrosst their respectable backs.

"Oh, these old things," says Marie, "They're jist somethin' the cat drug in."

"She don't mean that," says Reggie, "She's jist joshin' you. We're all real proud of our new git-ups!"

"We got us a bowlin' team, Danny," says Babe.

"This here's our outfits," says Marie which yanks at her pointed simply Gorgeous floppy collar.

"Glad you like 'em," says Babe to me, "My baby Lorraine designed 'em."

"Drink your Dr P, Danny," says Lorraine which turns red and shoots a kindly embarrassed look at Babe plus bends her head over contiguous and sings soft to me: "Little boy, you've had a busy day..."

Now ain't that a kind thing which to sing? Even although I am every item but little? Her Angel voice matches her Angel face Impeccable and she is singing a song which The Lonely Gal played on her radio program which instantaneously impels a unspecified number of tears to squirt out from my piglet 2 eyes. Big surprise. (Ha. Ha.)

Then I suddenly reminisce said Gal and oscillate my head around to find her. But her table is desserted!

"W-Where'd she g-go to?" I ask Babe which dips her red bandana in to a glass of ice water and swats my brows.

"She has went to get some sleep before her broadcast, Danny. She jist snuck off while you was sleepin'. But she'll be back tomorrow night at 7 PM 'cause it's Gala Talent Night and she's gonna sing a song she has wrote herself. You can come back then and hear her sing and meet her in person if she's sober."

"If he's able to," utters Lorraine. "You don't look real good, Danny boy. Maybe we should jist call your folks?"

I want to sink right on through the green Textile top on this pool table! OH MY GOSH! Am I Mortified! I peed myself and blubbered plus keeled over plus lost The Lonely Gal! Plus bus's tickets don't grow on no trees and I ain't got proficient funds to come back to Port City to see The Lonely Gal ever again as I hardly got funds left to purchase one battery for my battery radio! (Which is exceptionally low currantly.)

I slurp from my Dr P plus am nauseating Poste Haste.

"You oughta better lay back down agin, Danny boy," says Babe, "You've went all green!"

Lorraine grabs my Dr P glass and I lay back on to the pool table with my head on these smelling 2 bowling shoes which do not stink nearly so bad as prior as I am Fully Accustomized. However. I am currantly blue and lowly from said abrupt dessertion of The Lonely Gal.

From the corner of my eye I note Marie and Reggie which is playing their pool on the opposite segmant of this pool table Courteously so as to evade Disconcerting me. How Infinitely kind!

I feel a whole alots better untill a Bevy of pool balls comes whizzing acrosst said table and whizzes between the 2 bowling shoes and whacks me right on my head one after the other! Jist prior to when I pass out for the 2nd time I hear Reggie hollering: "FOR CHRIST'S SAKES, MARIE, WHAT HAVE YOU WENT AND DID?!"

Babe and Lorraine slaps me awake. What a wondrous feeling for one to have kind persons which care about you slapping us awake. A sore big bump has arosen through my red newly Revered Flaming hair.

Marie says that she is real sorry for braining me with her balls. I accept her apology gratuitously and insure her that worst items has occurred to me. (Such as PK Benderson) (ET. AL!) (To be Implicit!)

Reggie gives me a Milky-Way and Babe and Lorraine offers to drive me home in their blue beauteous 1941 Plymouth Convertible which was jist painted prior plus smells new. Babe and Lorraine has cut off the smashed roof of this auto which was wrecked with their Acetylene Torch theirselves which made it as good as new excepting for it's roof which is lacking.

"Who needs a car roof?" says Babe which is a Short Order cook plus enjoys spray painting in her spare time, "Hell, it never rains in Southern California!"

"And Lord knows," utters Lorraine which is a Reinforcement Engineer at Duff Mesh Wire Fences and a expert in Acetylene Torches and Bowling Shirts, "we got us a bitchin' car for a song!"

However. They keep a Tarpaulin in the trunk of this 1941 Plymouth jist in case of Reciprocation. Said Tarpaulin currantly lays right underneath of my damp heinie. (Jist in case.)

A excessively hot wind slams through Lemon Gulch tonight. The yellow shiny paint on The Big Lemon is flaking all over the darn place and shoots straight in to my piglet 2 eyes as we zoom past. Said Big Lemon is 8 feet tall and cement and is a monument to Lemon Gulch and sets in the middle of our town plus a tin sign which sits in front of it says:

LEMON GULCH
BEST CLIMATE IN THE COSMOS
COURTESY OF TANGY MAYONNAISE

Which is our town's biggest Statistical Employer. (As proudly prior said.)

Babe and Lorraine sing as we zoom along:

"I don't want no phony ro-mance
I don't want no triflin' love!
If your gonna be unfaithful
Get yourself another turtle-dove!"

Babe possesses a strong voice and is a fast but careful driver and I adore her more every time she is cussed out by variegated other drivers and pedestrians with fowl language.

"It ain't necessarily so!" she sings at said drivers and pedestrians as we zoom right along.

I lay on their Rear seat pronely underneath of a starry sky with my fat sausage 2 legs propped up on Babe and Lorraine's genuine leather bowling ball carrying bags and I am only a small bit uncomfortable due to said wetness of my Lower Pelvic Torsal Regions but I feel excessively content with my 2 kind and glamorous lady friends on who's satin black backs I read with exceptional joy:

"THE STEAMROLLERS"

The Best Climate In The Cosmos tin sign has became blowed off from The Big Lemon and lays on the road flopping up and down like a chicken with their head chopped off plus tangled up in a Tumbleweed. (A Dessert Growth.)

Babe jist misses the Best Climate sign with a real sharp swerve of our auto but only gets cussed-out for her efforts from a pedestrian which shouldn't of been loitering right in front of us in that darn pedestrian cross walk so late at night!

"It ain't necessarily so!" sings Babe right back at him as we zoom right by! Boy do we all laugh!

Babe and Lorraine kindly drive me up to the almost new Galvanized Wire Mesh gate of my home plus tells me that every fool plus their brother sporadically pees hisself sometimes and keels over which is a great comfort.

"And don't forget, Danny," utters Lorraine, "Gala Talent Night is tomorrow night at 7 PM."

I tell them that I will be there but I sadly do not ascertain how one can. I am real contented all the same as Babe and Lorraine likes me even although they ain't got no ideal that I am only 12 years of age and must ponder that I am 18 like most persons due to my inordinant height and growed-up Deportment. Anyhow. What a jolly Trio us 3 make!

I am Aghast when I ponder that I ain't even thunk of The Lonely Gal for about approximately a hour and a half precisely and she is the reason that I had went to Port City in the 1st darn place! I do not pride myself on this here Absent-Mindness.

I Dare Not to waddle through our front door as it is very late and Bull jist might be awake plus try to whack me with his phony leg so I climb through my bedroom window which is eternally unlocked plus ungarb and pee and climb on to my bed.

I have missed out on The Lonely Gal's radio program due to all of prior said plus am suddenly blue and lowly as I ain't got no ideal how to procure a bus's ticket for the trip to Gala Talent Night where I and The Lonely Gal can discuss our Humane Conditions In A Often Uncaring World after she has sang her song and is Leisurely Inclined.

However. I am exceedingly concerned on her Inebriation plus am so nerve racked that I ain't able to sleep so I reach way underneath of my bed for my traditional Peanut Oil and commence to ponder Fred Foster's weenie even although I am keeping it on my back burner.

After a Lubricious plus contenting Onanation I stick my Peanut Oil way back underneath of my bed and shift abruptly to Somnolence. Plus slumber sleepily.

ELSIE AND THE TRUTH

"I can't relax! I cannot relax! You of all...God! I was about to say "You of all *people* should know this!"

"You must try to relax, Elsie," he said.

She turned away, wincing with effort, in the very special chair. It had been delivered that morning, just before he arrived, in preparation for this event, this ordeal to come.

"You must lie back just the tiniest bit," he said, leaning toward her.

"I'm aching! Every inch of me aches! Can't you hear me?!"

"Yes, Elsie, I can hear you. But you must lie back just the tiniest bit so that we can make contact and I can --"

"Ease my pain?" she said quickly. "No! Not now, not yet. I have things to say. I must be very clear about the things I have to say. I must be precise."

"Of course, Elsie. But we can facilitate these things you have to say. Facilitate and simultaneously comfort you. That, of course, is our purpose. Let me continue."

"You must be aware of the conditions I stipulated when I signed on." She laughed. "When I signed *on* to...sign *off.*"

"Of course," he said.

"Then access your tiny electronic brain -- what do they call it?"

"My memory chip."

"Access that tiny memory chip of yours -- I shall call you Mr Chip. Access that miniscule memory chip of yours, Mr Chip, and you will find -- wonder of wonders -- that I suffer from --"

"That is not the point. We know well what you suffer from,

Elsie," he said. "What you, this minute, so needlessly, suffer from."

"Then I shall prefer to sit straight, keep my feet on the floor and my mind clear, if you don't mind!"

"But you must try to relax."

"It is the only way I can relax! I am increasingly astonished by the crudity of your approach."

"But I can ease your pain," he said. "Your suffering is useless, Elsie. It obstructs. I assumed our advisor had made that clear. Pain distorts. Makes our search more difficult. I will ease your pain. Then we can get on with it."

"No! Not yet," she said, pressing a button on the very special chair and moving what she assumed was a safer distance away.

"Let me activate," he said. "Watch my chest."

Elsie turned her eyes to his exquisitely sculptured chest as a large rectangle emerged between his two flashing, blue-lit nipples and became a shimmering mirror. In the mirror was her face. Her young, meltingly beautiful face. Her face of very long ago.

"Oh, God!" she cried, "What have you done with me?!"

Elsie could not take her eyes from his magical mirror and that happy self she had abandoned so very many years before. The mirror suddenly disappeared, her young face with it.

"Now make your mind a blank," he said. "Are you ready to proceed?"

"Yes, but may I see my young self again just once before we continue?"

"Of course. Soon. You must trust me. Do you trust me?"

"We shall see," she said.

"Say the first thing that comes into your mind. What do you think of when I say Love?"

"Good God! That technique is passé rubbish! Completely discarded well over a hundred years ago! Nothing in your offering said anything about such antiquated psycho-antics!"

"You must trust me," he broke in. "Free-Association has recently undergone a surprising renaissance. We shall continue. What do you think of when I say Love?"

"Enough! This is ridiculous! I submitted all required information for our...arrangement to every civil authority in Sydney! What have you been doing with your memory chip, Mr Chip? Playing naughty with yourself? I want my money back!"

"Please, Elsie, you must at least attempt to relax."

"I'm terminally ill!" cried Elsie. "Not mentally challenged! I am about to make a tiny telephone call. I am about to cancel my contract with you."

"That would be impossible," he said, We have just now orally reconfirmed that I am your facilitator, Elsie. And that your signature was lawfully obtained and duly witnessed. Our present event is legally registered and bound to reach its conclusion."

"Shall we continue?" he asked.

"Have I a choice?"

"No, my dear. Let us proceed. I see that you have two daughters. Is this correct?"

"Yes. Two. Regan and Goneril."

"Regan and Goneril? Are these not odd names for women?"

"My daughters are odd women, Mr Chip. They are named after the daughters of King Lear. I trust you've heard of William Shakespeare?! Or rather, your errant chip has heard of him?"

"Of course. Please continue."

"I had a third daughter. I could scarcely keep track of my progeny. My third daughter's name was, I believe, to have been Cordelia had she not died at birth. If Cordelia had lived I would not be speaking to you now. I would be speaking to Cordelia who would have loved me. Regan and Goneril do not love me. I have been a loving and self-sacrificing mother. Yet my two daughters do not love me."

"That is odd."

"So I said. Will you excuse me for a moment? I must take a pill."

"I can relieve you more efficiently than any pill, Elsie. I have the means."

"Absolutely not! I know about your means," she cried, and snapped open her small, silver bottle, shook out several tiny tablets, swallowed and washed them down with a glass of water from a lovely little hand-carved table by her side.

"Are you ready to continue?" he asked.

"Yes."

"Your husband left you eleven years ago."

"Like a thief in the night," she snapped. "Yes!"

This was not easy for Elsie and her face twisted as she said it. Her young face on Chip's mirror would have been little comfort just now -- until her tiny tablets took effect.

"Why did your husband leave you?"

"He was discontent."

"Like you?" said Chip.

"Not precisely, but I'll let that pass."

"Did he leave you for another woman?"

"Yes."

"Was she beautiful? This woman he left you for?"

"Ah! Such tact, Mr Chip. Yes, she was beautiful. And about a hundred years younger than I."

"Is he still with her?"

"I shouldn't think so -- not after she reached thirty. Which would have been...let me see, ah, yes! Her thirtieth birthday was a year ago. But, of course, I don't keep track of such things. April twenty-first. Yes, she would have reached thirty on April twenty-first, last year. But as I said..."

"You don't keep track of such things."

"Never!"

She smiled. Her tablets had begun to ease her and she said "The pain is a bit less now."

"During your marriage did you ever have an affair with another man?"

"Yes. Many. During my marriage and since. Many and often. I'm also terminally discontent, darling. Promiscuity is a strikingly signal symptom – pardon my alliteration – of terminal discontent. It is to be expected, is it not?"

"In certain cases," said Chip.

"But not mine? The joints of my fingers are so deformed that I cannot remove my wedding ring. Irony there."

"I am sorry."

"Sorry? I find it amusing," said Elsie.

"Something so painful cannot be amusing."

"Nature gets up to the damnedest tricks," smiled Elsie. "You wouldn't know about Nature, would you, Mr Chip?"

"Perhaps, Elsie, with more exhaustive programming."

"My daughter, Regan, will not allow me to visit her two children. She tells me I'd frighten them. Frighten my grandchildren with my deformed fingers."

"She has told you this?"

"Not in so few words," said Elsie. "I am very kind, you must know from my papers. Perhaps not a model Granny but... My discomfort is easing somewhat."

"So you said earlier."

"Did I?"

"But I can help you…"

"No. My pills are not perfect but I must know I am still alive. My own pills will do. Just now."

"Yes," agreed Chip with a perfect, empathetic smile.

"I am very kind in my way," said Elsie, gazing at her young, exceptionally beautiful self that had just reappeared in Chip's shimmering mirror.

Comforted, she said "I was a model Granny."

"I'm sure you were. And your other daughter, Goneril?"

"I never see her."

"Why?"

"She is discontent."

"Everyone, it seems, is discontent."

"Hurrah!" laughed Elsie, "The penny drops at last!" She laughed again but stopped short. "Discontent is the stuff that dreams are made of. I nurse my discontent. I husband it. Pardon my pun. It can move mountains. Has. My daughters are monsters."

"I do not believe you."

"I pay you to believe me!"

"But you are lying, Elsie. It will not help you. Lying is not the purpose of our --"

"So sorry, Mr Chip. I shall endeavour to stifle my mythomaniacal impulses. My daughters are lovely women. Their names are Briony and Caitlin. Briony has a beautiful little girl named Marianne, and Caitlin is pregnant with a son to be called Kevin, after Caitlin's husband. My daughters are wonderful to me but I'm afraid I'm not much help to them. My hands. I wish you could see my hands."

"Take off your gloves, please."

She removed her gloves with some effort, held up her fingers. "There. Shocked? Are they not grotesque? I am being destroyed. Obliterated, finger by finger."

"Watch now, Elsie, in my mirror."

Elsie buzzed herself closer, peered anxiously into Chip's magical mirror as her hands replaced her lovely young face. "My hands! As they were! Perfect! Elegant! Thank you, Mr Chip. You have done wonders with me."

"Let us proceed," said Chip.

"Gladly, darling. I'll soldier on! When my husband left I was suicidal. No. Not really. Who am I kidding? No. Not at all. Nil. Nix. I was happy to see him go. He didn't love me anymore. He loved her. Her name is Frances. His name is Francis. I wish them eternal confusion," continued Elsie, "She was in films for a while – kind of, you know, *fleshed* them out. I mentioned that she was many years younger than I?"

"Yes."

"But I had my friends too. Francis and I were never a model of propriety. Or perhaps, in our way, we were. When he left I was not surprised or even disappointed. Only suicidal."

Elsie laughed, pulled on her gloves, noted happily that her perfect hands had now been replaced by her young face in Chip's magic mirror. "Suicidal for five minutes! He left me this flat of course. Rather nice, isn't it?" She laughed.

"Yes."

"In its way. The sale of the furniture alone could support me for the rest of my life. Whoops! Not saying much for the furniture, is it? He provided a substantial income too – he'll be so relieved. What time is it? Am I...?"

"You have time, Elsie."

"Goody. Oh, yes. I have far more than an adequate income and a lovely, huge car that I can no longer drive. A friend of mine – intimate friend of mine used to drive me about. Used to drive me about till my fingers became so deformed I couldn't get my fabulous diamond off." Elsie's young face twisted in Chip's magic mirror. "Not that his driving was in any way responsible for my fingers but..." she smiled, "he had rather counted on that diamond, poor man. He had serious plans for that diamond. This was, of course, before diamonds became common as gravel."

Elsie removed her left glove, a gigantic diamond glittered on her ring finger. "See? I'll hold it close. A quite perfect blue, isn't it?"

"Yes. Perfect."

"He intended to sell it. I wouldn't let him – not only, of course, because I couldn't get it off my goddamned finger -- and I use that finger-adjective advisedly. I do believe he might have taken the finger as well. Fortunately, I've never been a heavy sleeper." Elsie sighed. "I go nowhere now, in my huge car. I could hire a chauffeur but I can't be bothered. Can you drive, Mr Chip?"

"No."

"Lots of people who can't, do."

"Yes."

"In any case, it's better that I stay in, isn't it? Briony and Caitlin ring me constantly. I'm surprised they haven't rung today. Oh, yes! Caitlin has been selected by a prominent designer of footwear to model their new line. Gets all her shoes free too, gives me millions of pairs. I've got enough shoes to walk me -- if I could walk -- to the end of the world... whoops! Irony there too! Caitlin will be very busy just now. It's her feet, you see. She has the smallest feet on earth. Inherited directly from me. So my tiny-footed daughter, bless her, won't be ringing today. She'll be modelling footwear. Hurrah!"

"But Caitlin is pregnant," said Chip.

"It doesn't show yet. Besides, they only photograph her from the ankles down – God, you're picky! Though you do take me out of myself."

"That is my purpose," grinned Chip.

"You smile nicely, Mr Chip. With a little practice you could conquer the neighbourhood. The grinning Grim Reaper! How are we for time? Am I running late?"

"Not at all. Please go on," said Chip. "You do take me out of myself."

"My hired machine has a sense of humour!" laughed Elsie. "But Briony. Why hasn't Briony rung?"

"Little Marianne keeps her very busy," said Chip.

"Yes. She spoils the child, really. But so do I. I am the original doting grandma," cooed Elsie, gazing serenely at her young other-self in Chip's magic mirror. Then suddenly: "I've had enough of this stupid game-playing!" she cried, twisting painfully in the very special chair. "Goddamn it! I need a pill! Tell me a story and I'll take my pills." Elsie shook several tiny tablets into her hand, took up a glass of water.

"I can ease your pain, Elsie. Please let me help you."

"No! In the interests of clarity, no," said Elsie who swallowed her tiny tablets and set down her glass and said "Tell me a story, Mr Chip."

"Gladly," said Chip. "There was once a distinguished, extremely beautiful and intelligent woman --"

"Yes. That's it. That's the one!"

"This distinguished, extremely beautiful and intelligent woman had no daughters. She had no husband although many prominent, eligible men would have wished it otherwise. She preferred a career instead. A career devoted to the service of others. She was a magnificently gifted brain surgeon..."

"Yes. I like this, Mr Chip. I love this story."

"...a magnificently gifted brain surgeon who sat comfortably --"

"Ah. To sit comfortably again," sighed Elsie.

"This extremely beautiful brain surgeon sat comfortably at the very pinnacle of her profession and, much sought after, flew to and fro amongst the major capitals of the world treating worthy and wealthy citizens right and left."

"Yes," cried Elsie. "To and fro! Right and left! Oh, yes!"

"Her invaluable expertise was equally available to the poor. For she often worked weeks at a time on destitute unfortunates from whom she had no hope of payment."

"That's me! Oh, yes, that's me! Oh, continue!"

"This utterly devoted, singular woman was honorary president of a dozen philanthropic organizations and influenced many wise and merciful decisions which led to better lives for thousands the world over."

"Oh yes! Yes! Yes! Yes!"

"Then..."

"Then? No! that's enough!" cried Elsie.

"Then...then," said Chip, "she was struck down by --"

"Stop! Stop! Have you no heart?!"

"No," said Chip. "I do not."

"Why hasn't Briony rung me?"

"She is busy with little Marianne."

"Who is Marianne?"

"Your grandchild," said Chip.

"Oh. Yes," said Elsie, a lovely, angelic child."

"Tell me about your husband, Elsie."

"Which husband? I've had four. Which husband? They were all thieves in the night. Thieves of love. Oh. Have I said that before?"

"I believe..." said Chip

"But so what?!" she added angrily as her young face disappeared from Chip's mirror. "I want me back," said Elsie. Put me back, Mr Chip."

"Tell me, Elsie, about the one you loved. The one husband you loved."

"Loved?!" Elsie threw back her head and laughed.

"My memory file tells me --" began Chip.

"Stuff your memory file! Stuff it!"

Elsie nearly rose from her very special chair. She cried "OUCH!" and sat up straight and tried to reach her left ankle and screamed "WHAT THE HELL WAS THAT?!"

"We have made contact, Elsie. Now we can help you. Tell me about the husband you loved."

Elsie's meltingly beautiful young self now reappeared in Chip's magical mirror. Elsie was exultant.

"Ah yes!" she cried happily. "The husband I loved. His name was Teddy. Teddy for Theodore. Ginger hair had Teddy. And freckles. His nose was simply one large freckle, snubbed heavenward. Skin like rosy peaches. He worked at the medical library. I was still at university so I was constantly in and out of the library – studying my...my brain surgery. Teddy was at the front desk. I went to inquire about a certain scientific treatise – or should that be thesis?"

"Either. It depends," said Chip.

"Yes. Of course," said Elsie. "Doesn't it always?"

"I hope our contact was not too abrupt or unpleasant."

"Actually, I am feeling quite pleasant. Even serene," said

Elsie whose face now shone with a relief not experienced in, what seemed to her, forever.

"So here I was at the front desk and there was Teddy," sighed Elsie, remembering. "Teddy looked up. Our eyes met. I inquired about that scientific treatise or thesis. Teddy looked down, consulting his lists. My heart pounded so hard I feared he might see it through my cardigan. Teddy looked up. I thought I would die! Brain surgery he said, *brain* surgery? Teddy looked down to recheck his member list because I was so young. I grasped the desk for support! Teddy looked up. I was in love! And Teddy… Teddy was in love with me!"

Elsie laughed happily for a moment and was suddenly silent, staring at her slowly disappearing image in Chip's mirror. "I don't feel well, Mr Chip. I don't feel well, Mr Machine. I don't feel well…"

"Perhaps it was something you ate?" offered Chip, helpfully, not wishing to admit it was possible he'd over-prescribed her dose level at contact.

"No, dear," said Elsie. "It was something I did -- didn't -- do. A millennium ago."

"Would you care to tell me what it was you did -- didn't -- do?"

"No. Yes. No. And now I've forgotten. A story, Mr Chip? Please? May I have another story?"

"Gladly, Elsie. There was once a young woman who was extraordinarily beautiful and kind. But exceptionally vulnerable. Her mother had run away with another man and this young beautiful…"

"Yes," whispered Elsie.

"This young, beautiful, kind and exceptionally vulnerable woman was forced to live alone with her cruel father. A father so cruel that when this young woman was but a child of fourteen her cruel father punished her for painting her nails pink, by dipping her fingertips into a jar of lye."

"Yes," whispered Elsie.

"When this young, exceptionally vulnerable woman reached the age of sixteen she forsook her cruel father and fled with a youth of eighteen. He soon deserted her and she found herself alone and destitute in a strange city a thousand miles from her home."

"Yes," whispered Elsie. "It is true."

"As chance would have it, this was the selfsame city to which her mother had decamped three years before and, quite by accident, on the street the two women met. The young, beautiful, kind and exceptionally vulnerable woman flung herself into her mother's arms but the mother, not recognising her, thrust her away. Mother! Mother! cried the young woman, Mother, it is I!"

"Oh! Yes! Yes! But no! Oh, No!" gasped Elsie.

"The mother, recognising her daughter at last, wept suitably for a moment then asked the girl home to tea. After they'd had tea and talked for an hour the mother excused herself and, saying she had a terrible headache, left her daughter in the company of a man whom she, the mother, had recently met at a party. This man immediately made an indecent proposal and the poor girl fled, yet again, poor young thing, into the night."

"Poor thing. Poor, poor young thing," sighed Elsie.

"The stricken girl ran wildly, abandoned to tears, and found herself some time later beside the imposing entrance of a large stadium, amidst hundreds of shouting, laughing, uncouth people. Caught in this whirlpool of mankind, she was sucked into its vortex up, up, up onto a high terrace of seats where she saw, far below her in a pool of smoky yellow light, a boxing ring in which two men were about to engage in what was to be a savage round of pugilism."

A distant start bell clanged in Elsie's head. A crowd cheered and applauded.

"The frightened girl was perplexed," continued Chip. "She had never seen a boxing match and the savagery of her father paled beside it. She wiped her eyes and squinted and was able to make out the lithe form of one of the boxers far below."

"Oh yes! Yes!" cheered Elsie, "the lithe form!"

"The poor vulnerable child was instantly struck by this exciting young man's strength and utter commitment. She was abruptly enchanted and fell in love with him in less than one minute."

"Love is like that, isn't it, Mr Chip?" sighed Elsie. "Love is wonderful, isn't it?"

"Far below," continued Chip. "Far below in that circle of smoky, yellow light, as though he had felt the surge of her astonishing affection from above, the lithe, powerful and committed young man lifted his golden head toward this fully infatuated, utterly beautiful young woman and was immediately punched in his jaw and knocked senseless."

"He had a glass jaw, didn't he?!" cried Elsie. "Yes!"

"The first thing he saw upon regaining his senses was the shining face of the deeply devoted, young, beautiful, kind, and exceptionally vulnerable young woman who had valiantly made her way into the unconscious boxer's changing room."

"I was kind! I was beautiful! I was vulnerable yet valiant! Yes! Yes! And I was young!" cried Elsie.

"And," said Chip, they lived happily ever after."

"Did they?" said Elsie, who, startled, turned painfully in her very special chair as the telephone rang beside her.

"It's Briony! My dearest daughter, Briony! It must be Briony!" cried Elsie and snatched up the telephone. "Briony, darling?!... Who?...No."

Elsie slammed down the telephone, said "Wrong number."

"Briony is too busy with the child, Marianne," said Chip.

"Marianne?"

"Your daughter's child, Marianne."

"Yes, of course. And Caitlin is much too involved with her modeling..."

"Shoes," said Chip.

"Yes. Her tiny feet that she inherited from me got her that job. Shoes always look better on tiny feet."

"And your daughters, Regan and Goneril?" said Chip.

"Darling Mr Chip, Regan and Goneril were daughters of King Lear."

"Sorry, Elsie. My mistake."

Elsie, who was in much better spirits, sang out "Pill time!" and was about to snap open her bottle of tablets when Chip said "You must allow me to assist you, Elsie. Your tablets are unnecessary now we have made contact."

"Sorry, Mr Chip. My memory is a sieve today."

"Think nothing of it, dear Elsie. A very human failing."

"So was my life, it seems. A very human failing. What was it like, my life, my life with the boxer?"

"You can answer that better than I," said Chip.

"I should know. When a person dies it is said their whole life passes before their eyes. Clear as crystal."

"You are in error, Elsie. When a person drowns their whole life passes before their eyes. One must be drowning."

"I am drowning. Clear as crystal. What was life like with my boxer? My...pugilist? Well, Mr Chip, we fought a lot."

Elsie laughed. "But we managed, intra-bellum to procreate. Two beautiful daughters who were Mummy's pride and great joy. One married a prince, the other, an oil baron who was the prince's fabulously wealthy associate. Both daughters and their husbands were killed in a coup in that prince's high desert country. But we can't mourn forever, can we?"

"No, Elsie. We can't. Nor should we."

"Of course," continued Elsie, "the deaths of his two daughters killed the...boxer. But he had been drinking a great deal in any case and his health had broken – like mine. He died six weeks later of grief and a liver disease brought on by his excesses. It was a blessing. We can't mourn forever."

"Apparently not."

"Ah. Mr Chip! Have you been pulling unseen levers

beneath that glamorously shiny exterior of yours? My pills were not half so effective as --"

"Since contact, Elsie, our procedure has been swimmingly automatic -- programmed to sense deeply buried anxieties you are not aware of, and to correct them and provide maximal comfort."

"Your company must be very proud of you, darling. You are quite handsome in a metallic sort of way."

"Thank you, Elsie."

"I adore your little coloured lights, especially the little blue ones at the tip of your delicious chromium nipples. Do those little coloured lights have a function? Or are they merely... decorative? For effect?"

"Decorative, Elsie. But, I think, effective."

"You're vain. Rather like me, my dear," said Elsie. "My legs are quite shapely but merely for effect. They don't walk anymore." Elsie pulled her skirt up to her knees.

"You legs are lovely, Elsie. Shall I feature them on our little mirror?

"No, darling, not *today*," she sighed and almost smiled. Your... associates, Mr Chip, they will come –– they will come and fetch me when...?"

"Yes, Elsie."

"I do not wish my daughters inconvenienced in any way."

"No one will be inconvenienced. We have plenty of time."

"How much time?"

"Enough, dear Elsie."

"May I see my young face and my beautiful hands again?"

"Of course, Elsie, at the right time."

"I loved your ad. I liked your presentation. All your special features; the image of my face, younger of course, on your screen. Your price was right. Though I could easily have afforded several others – I compared all the cyber-brochures, you know. But I adored your little blue lights. Is that what everything boils down to, Mr Chip? Little coloured lights?

Will I feel it, dear? When the time comes, will I feel it? All the brochures say you won't. But I know one does – I mean if one chooses to remain conscious as of course I have stipulated. Will I feel it?"

"Not unless you wish to, Elsie."

"How will you do it?"

"I am not at liberty to --"

"Sorry, Mr Chip."

"You are well apprised of the terms of our contract."

"I said I was sorry! Jesus! Hang me at sunset! You remind me of Teddy the librarian! Prim and precise! You'll drive me mad! You machines are all alike! I once had three robo-gardeners and a cook! You're all alike! Picky bastards, all!"

"I have just raised your comfort level, Elsie, dear. You will feel it momentarily."

"Ah!" sighed Elsie. "I do feel it, darling, my knight in shining, stainless steel. But can one feel it when ones soul slips away? Assuming one has a soul. Is there some colossal, white, friendly glow beckoning us? Some super-sun sucking us into it? It does seem far too easy. We should be made to fight for the peace of the grave."

"My info-file informs me that you are to be cremated. What is this grave you refer to? It is not in our contract."

"You machines are so literal, darling. Tell me another story. Your stories are so much more exciting than mine."

"Gladly, Elsie. There was once a clever young woman. She had only recently begun university but was an instant success. Not necessarily as a scholar. For her intellectual achievement was merely somewhat more than adequate. But with her fellow students she was a star. Everyone loved her, men and women alike. They were attracted by her easy laughter and her crackling wit and her manner of looking at the world in the oddest way. She's one in a million! said a close acquaintance named Edward. They broke the mould after they made Jean Morgan! said a girlfriend. And --"

"Her name was Jean Morgan?" said Elsie.

"Perhaps," said Chip. "Jean was the kindling spark of every party. Always at the very center of every ripple of laughter that erupted round her ring of friends. They laughed and laughed at Jean's manner of looking at the world in the oddest way."

"What do you mean, Mr Chip? Looking at the world in the oddest way?"

"Jean didn't take the world seriously. She was in it but not of it."

"Oh! But that's me!" cried Elsie.

"Jean laughed at her misfortune," said Chip.

"Misfortune? Jean doesn't sound unfortunate to me."

"But she was. If misfortune is to be measured in loneliness."

"But she was surrounded! She was positively suffocating in good will! The spoiled cow! Everybody loved her!"

"Everybody in general. But nobody in particular," said Chip.

"Jee-sus!" snapped Elsie, "Jesus H. Christ!"

"Your level of comfort has just been raised again, Elsie, dear. May we continue?"

"Ah! Thank you, my dearest, my darling Mr Chip! Bliss! I now float yet higher on this frothy wave of pleasure you so unselfishly provide. Pain is but a distant enemy. But may I see my young self again, betwixt your winking blinking, blue lights? May I, my dear little tin woodsman?"

"In due course, Elsie. Do you remember Edward?"

"Yes. He said he had to go to the loo and left me. He didn't say the loo was in Singapore. I know this story. I do not like this story. Please desist."

"Jean's odd ways became odder. For years she was in and out of mental hospitals and various institutions," said Chip.

"I do not like this story, Mr Chip, Please tell me another story."

"I am getting a message from my file. Elsie. How many

husbands have you had? I note a discrepancy."

"I could not remember my husband's names when I – when your employee – filled in my application for your services. You won't, therefore, have all their names. Is that clear enough? Am I in any condition to be clearer? Your information specifically promised kind assistance in the search for Truth. Is there not one promise in this whole sodding world that can be kept?!"

"I shall be happy to describe your nameless husbands according to your --"

"No. I shall. You'll have Teddy's name. Yes, you'll have that dear little librarian's name. And, of course, Francis. Of Francis and Frances."

"Husband One: Father of Regan and Goneril. Husband Two: The boxer. His name?" said Chip.

"Haven't a clue, darling. He cried when our two daughters perished in that coup in high desert country. He died very soon after. Of a broken heart."

"Six weeks after, to be exact," said Chip.

"You can't mourn forever."

"No."

"But he may have been husband one, darling. Can't help you there.

"Husband three. His name?" said Chip.

"Possibly, just possibly, Teddy the librarian. As I don't believe we married instantly, the day he located that brain surgery treatise for me – or should that be thesis? I was at that time only sixteen and a half. A sixteen and a half year old, brain-surgical prodigy. Oh! Now I remember! Teddy was the father of Regan and Goneril! I was so forgetful when I – your employee actually – filled in my application for your services."

"We shall forget chronological order," said Chip.

"Why not? What does it matter? One thing inevitably follows another anyway, doesn't it?"

"We shall forget chronological order," he repeated.

"Mr Chip, is all this really necessary?"

"It is for the others, Elsie. Your loved ones."

"And who might they be? -- Oh. *Them!*" cried Elsie.

"For posterity."

"We shall forget chronological order and simply state your liaisons. They need not be blessed..."

"Blessed, darling?!" Elsie laughed.

"With matrimony."

"Matrimony is a blessing?" laughed Elsie.

"Who was the father of Briony and Caitlin?" said Chip.

"Haven't the foggiest. He just slipped right in there where it counted. Sorry. I fear my memory has not kept pace with my ancient activities. I have had a very complicated life – a messy life, if you will."

"All lives are messy, Elsie."

"Was mine messier than most?"

"No. Your life is simple if the truth be told."

"Ah! That nasty old truth! Then tell it, dearest robot! Tell it! Forget our little fantasy games and tell me the truth!"

"Based upon your application for our services --"

"I could have lied. Did lie."

"Based upon your application and our interview to present," continued Chip.

"Stop! First let me tell you about yourself. Have I time? My impressions, one hopes, are still valid? Even at this relatively late date, valid?"

"Based upon your application, the validated medical reports of your condition and what I have observed thus far in our interview..." continued Chip.

"Let me, first, describe what I see in you, Mr Chip, my hired assassin, whilst I metaphorically walk to the end of our world on my truly tiny, still attractive, though utterly unusable feet."

"Based upon our --"

"Shut up, darling! One: You are shiny. In a cheap but not unattractive way. Two: I do not like this very special chair your company provided. Three: Nor this...odd little plastic cord, that I have only recently discovered around my ankle. Though it is heated to body temperature it is comfortable but mysterious."

"One might say it is our umbilical cord. It is attached to your special chair, dear Elsie, and I too am, through the air, attached to your chair."

"Ah! Through the air, attached to my chair comes the rhyming angel of death. Are we Siamese twins, now, Mr Chip? With but one lethal purpose?"

"I must have access to your --"

"My bloodstream, Mr Chip?

"Yes, dearest Elsie, if I am to help you."

"It is not pleasant, Mr Chip, your 'umbilical' chord in reverse, with its fang-like bracelet. I have no idea when you attached it to me. Did it creep from the innards of my very special chair? Or did it leap from you?"

"But what do you *like* about me?" asked Chip. "Your saviour should not go unappreciated."

"My saviour?! My assassin as saviour? Ah. So that's your nasty little secret. Whose bible have you been reading? Well, dear Mr Chip -- about you. As I said, I particularly like your little blue lights. I particularly like the lovely image of my own young face on your magic mirror. This damsel in distress is at least, at the last, briefly alluring. Thank you for that. You have also kindly reshaped my poor fingers in your magic mirror whenever I brought them into your range. Thank you. I like, for the most part, your stories."

"My stories, Elsie, are based on..."

"Quiet, darling! I dislike you for not having a proper sense of humour, and for having no heart. I pity you for not being human. We humans have all the fun, haven't we? Even as you wrest the world from our grasp we humans are still having all the fun."

Elsie, smiled, attempted to twist her 'contact' ankle to a

more comfortable position.

"Now it's your turn," she said. "The truth! Let's have it! Fire away!"

"Which truth do you desire, Elsie?"

"The truth, you pretentious tin box! I'm paying a fortune for this final analysis! I want my money's worth. I want...I want...Oh jesus! I'm hurting! I'm not supposed to hurt, Mr Chip!"

"With deepest sympathy, Elsie, I must ask again: Which truth do you desire?"

"To be free of pain. Completely free of pain!"

"Then that is the truth. The whole truth. Nothing but the truth."

"Yes. Yes. The rest is immaterial. Window dressing," whispered Elsie.

"We have raised your comfort level to maximum, Elsie. It is nearly time. We dared not raise it before."

"Thank you, Mr Chip. I'm ready, darling."

"You are certain?"

"Oh yes! I feel... glorious! Is that not appropriate?"

"You have read and agreed to clauses one, two and three, page one of our agreement?"

"Yes."

"You are being recorded."

"Yes. For posterity, darling Mr Chip."

"All affairs are in order?"

"Possibly not in the correct order. But in order. Yes," said Elsie.

"The disposal of your personal property and real property?"

"What's real, Mr Chip?"

"This luxurious apartment."

"Yes. The flat is real enough though I do occasionally have serious doubts about the plumbing," laughed Elsie.

"You have instructed the disposal of all properties? – refer to page four -- and have signed your name in all cases?

We ask only because we need your oral confirmation of all documents."

"Yes to all, darling. Just a moment, Mr Chip, I must put my telephone on automatic answering. Briony or Caitlin might ring."

Elsie set a switch on the telephone at her elbow.

"And of course they will be informed after the fact," said Chip.

"Oh? After the fact? Suddenly I'm a fact? As important as all that? Oh, Mr Chip! I'm flattered. When will it happen, darling?"

"It has already happened, Elsie."

"When?"

"A moment ago," said Chip.

"I didn't notice, dear."

"No."

"But will I know?" said Elsie, "Will I know when my... what-ever-it-is, my soul-thingy, slips away? Takes flight, as it were? As Jean's did. As Jean's immortal soul did when she jumped."

"We cannot guarantee anything," said Chip, "We cannot guarantee anything but the serene peace of the --"

"I did not want to live after Jean died. Jean was everything to me. She pushed my chair about, you see, not this chair, this chair frightens me. Jean listened to my complaints. There were many. She read to me. Are you listening?"

"Yes, Elsie."

"I could see that night, from my window," Elsie motioned, "that window. I could see...push me to the window, Mr Chip."

Chip clicked, buzzed very slightly, rose and pushed Elsie's chair across the huge, luxuriously appointed room to the window so she could look out.

"I can see Jean," said Elsie, "just now, climbing the steps to the railway bridge. Can you see her too, Mr Chip?"

"Yes," said Chip, though he could not, "Yes, Elsie, dear.

There she is."

"I can hear a train coming now. Can you? Can you hear the train coming?"

"Yes. Yes, darling Elsie, I can hear the train."

"Oh, I'm so glad, dearest Mr Chip! It's coming for me, too, isn't it? The train is coming for me too."

"Yes, my dear. Are you comfortable? Is there anything I can --"

"Hush, Mr Chip. See? There is Jean. She has been out for her evening walk. She always took an evening walk, smoked a cigarette, took her time. Perhaps she met someone during her evening walks, someone else to chat with – I don't know. It did Jean good to get away from me for a while. I was not always easy to be with though I cared deeply for Jean. I suppose she was, in a way -- no, in all ways -- the great love of my life. She amused me. Strange how two lives entwine. Strange how I became her and she became me. Strange, isn't it, Mr Chip?"

"Not at all, Elsie."

"Jean's wit transported me. Her smile was breathtaking. Of course, she had, as I do, the oddest way of looking at the world. Funny how a life can boil down to just one other person. I could see her quite clearly that night on the railway bridge. There is a lamp directly over the centre of the bridge, see it, Mr Chip? It was in its circle of light that Jean would stand and smoke a last cigarette before she returned each night. It was easy for me, even at that distance to see it was Jean. She wore a beret, you see. A beret like something out of an old French film," Elsie laughed, "and a trench coat! Imagine that! Like Humphrey Bogart. But our Mr Chip wouldn't know Humphrey Bogart from a hill of beans, would he? Would you, Mr Chip? Mr Chip off the old whatever."

"Elsie, I --"

"Hush, darling! Oh, my...I'm feeling a bit...just the tiniest bit something-or-other. Never mind. Never mind, dear. So there I was -- I always watched from my window as Jean had her last cigarette there at the middle of the railway bridge. Yes! Yes! See! There she is now! She has reached the circle of light! There is my Jean! Oh, Jean, you mustn't!"

"Please relax, Elsie, dear," soothed Chip.

"Yes, of course, darling. I'll relax soon enough. It was a purplish-black evening – like tonight.. Precisely like tonight. Jean leaned over that bridge-railing far below in her halo of golden light – like my champion boxer, my prize-fighter, what was his name? Never mind. There she stood, my Jean Morgan in her halo of gold in that great purple darkness, a nocturne in purple and gold like a Whistler painting. Was it like Whistler, Mr Chip?"

"I am so sorry, dearest Elsie. Without more exhaustive programming I am not --"

"Hush, dear! Neither am I. She was so very small down there on the bridge but I knew it was Jean. Then..." said Elsie, and her voice began to slur. "...Then Jean started to climb over the railing... No! No! Jean! Don't! Stop her! Mr Chip! Please stop her!"

"It is too late, Elsie."

A shrieking train whistle blared in her head as Elsie turned her tear-flooded face from the window, peered at Chip. "Could Jean feel it when her soul took wing? Could she feel that exhilarating separation of spirit from flesh? She wasn't there, Mr Chip. She wasn't there when the train...finalized her. As you have finalized me. No. She'd gone! Been... gone... for some time... Oh, my, darling Chip," slurred Elsie, nearing sleep. "I'm feeling a bit more something-or-other. Jean read to me, you see. You do see? Told me stories, as you did."

"Yes."

"I've enjoyed our little talk, Mr...Chip, is it? Is that you? Are you... *my* Mr Chip?"

"Yes, Elsie, I am."

"I have enjoyed our... little talk."

"So have I, dearest Elsie."

"I'm drowning now... darling. In the pleasantest possible way. Oh, my. All rather confusing, wasn't it? My life? Not an ounce of truth to it...was there? Wasn't crystal-clear at all, was it? Didn't make much sense...my life, did it?"

"They never do, Elsie, make much sense."

"I love your coloured lights, darling, especially those delicious little... blue ones. May I see my lovely young self once more, dear?"

"Certainly, Elsie, my dearest."

"Oh! Thank you, darling..." Elsie peered sleepily into Chip's mirror. "Was I good company... my sweet? Was I...simply... captivating? I adore...machines. Humans were never much help, you know, in the...long run. Oh! I can't see me now. Are you still there, darling? I seem to be...experiencing some... fleeting problem with...my eyes. But..."

"Yes, Elsie."

"Goodbye...Goodbye. Goodbye, Mr Chip -- please... do pardon my...droll sense... of humour... darling," sighed Elsie and was still.

"Goodbye, Elsie," whispered Chip just as her telephone rang and was automatically answered: "To whom it may concern," sang Elsie's lilting, laughing voice, "You've reached a disconnected number."

Chip felt wetness on his face. A manufacturing flaw no doubt. He clicked himself off and the tears stopped.

The company would soon come for them both -- Elsie, to be delivered to the city morgue, Chip, to his next assignment.

RESCUING VERA AND NOLA

(excerpt from the novel, OUR YANK, 2011)

It was morning when Andy jerked straight up in his bed, wiped his eyes, felt his head. It ached. It hammered! Then he heard a faint "Yoooooooo-hoooooo!"

Was it coming from his basement window? No. It was drifting down the basement stairs. "Yoooooo-hoooooooo!"

"Well I think it's disgraceful, Vera," said Nola, at the third floor landing outside hers and Vera's double bed-sitter. "Disgraceful! And me and you with our knees!"

"Not to worry, love. She'll come. She always does, sooner or later."

"Later, more like," sniffed Nola.

Vera, too, was now on her cane at their open door. "Yooooo-hooooo!" she cried down the staircase, "Yoooo-hooo!"

"Well she's not coming!" said Nola, "and that's a fact! It's a disgrace. Us with no heat and these knees!"

Vera left the door and hobbled on her cane to a covered birdcage. "We'll play with Harry whilst we wait. He'll have his morning lesson, won't he?"

Vera took the cloth from the birdcage, Nola followed.

"Good morning, Harry," said Vera.

"Good morning, Harry," said Nola.

"I'll put on his lesson, dear," said Vera.

"Do," said Nola. "But it will be in vain. You know very well budgerigars seldom speak properly. I have said this again and again but to no avail. Oh, I know when you buy them they always say they'll talk -- keep you company, recite the bleedin' Magna Carta but they never do. I told you, dear.

- 134 -

These mediocre, cheap ones never do. They never do."

"Harry will, sooner or later," said Vera, "We've only had him a week, love."

She switched on a turntable, pushed it close beside the birdcage and set a record on and turned the volume to maximum. A low and booming voice, obviously at the wrong and slowest turntable's speed began:

"HELLLL-OOOOOO, BABY! WANT A KISS?!"

"His lesson record was dearer than he was," said Nola, "We were duped."

From his basement room Andy cocked his ear towards his door which 'bloodshot' had left cracked slightly open and heard "HELLLL-OOOOOO, BABY! WANT A KISS?!"

Then: "Yoooo-hooooooo! Can anybody help two damsels in distress?! It's our knees!" came echoing down the stairs from the top of the house.

Ever the gentleman, Andy groggily pulled on his trousers and that dead man's robe, sneezed twice, had a brief though thoughtful reprise of something not quite known but, anyhow, pleasant from the night before. He wondered why breakfast had not arrived, and climbed, coughing, head hammering with fever, from his bed to rescue a prospective damsel in distress.

Here stood Andy, shivering in a cold sweat, at the top of their landing. There were two of them. Two damsels in distress.

"It's Iris!" called Nola from her chair before the unlit gas fire.

"Yes, it's Iris!" said Vera, leaning on her cane in the door, "She's forgot our gas meter again."

"It's not the first time," called Nola.

"Nor, I fear, will it be the last," said Vera.

Andy's hangover headache was pounding and a billion cold-germs pulsed through his shivering frame. He stood in the door waiting for a loophole to speak. He required larger loopholes than average. It took him time to get his words together. The continuing repetition of the booming voice of Harry the budgerigar's speech lesson, "HELLL-OOOOO, BABY, WANT A KISS?!" was not helping either.

"We've not yet had our breakfast tea and our gas fire's gone off!" said Vera, balancing precariously on her cane and pulling her trim, lavender cardigan closer around her stooped shoulders.

"HELLL-OOOOO, BABY, WANT A KISS?!" boomed the recording at the wrong speed-setting.

"It's our knees, you see," moaned Nola.

"It's sheer agony replenishing our meters on our own," said Vera, "All those stairs!"

"It's a disgrace!" moaned Nola.

"And poor Gladys being blind and all," said Vera, "had to tap her way down to the basement last night!"

"It's disgraceful!" said Nola.

"HELLL-OOOOO, BABY, WANT A KISS?!"

"I l-live in the b-basement," said Andy, "I'll t-take care of your m-meters."

"Oh, would you, dear?" said Vera.

"HELLL-OOOOO, BABY, WANT A KISS?!"

Tiny Harry the budgerigar, was as usual terrified by his lesson record and had shrunk, shivering, as far as possible against the opposite side of his birdcage, his green and yellow tail feathers poking askew through the cage wires.

"HELLL-OOOOO, BABY, WANT A KISS?!"

"Your r-record is on the wrong s-speed," said Andy, wiping a shimmering splash of cold sweat from his brow, "You've g-got it on l-long-play m-mode. It's a 78 rpm, isn't it?"

"I don't know what you're talking about, dear," said Vera, a bit guiltily as she dug deep into her lavender cardigan pockets for shillings, "But you must be right."

"Of course he's right," snapped Nola. Yanks know about these technology things. I always did think Harry's lesson sounded peculiar."

"Well, I wish you'd said, Nola, dear. You know I'm quite tone deaf," said Vera, again somewhat guiltily.

Obviously, something was up. Something only Vera herself knew about.

"HELLL-OOOOO, BABY, WANT A KISS?!"

Nola rose painfully from her chair before the unlit gas fire and led Andy, by his elbow, to the gramophone. "Do the honours, love," she said, and he adjusted the record to its proper speed, as Vera stood by smiling a very reluctant -- it seemed to Andy -- smile.

"Oh that's much better, dear!" cried Nola, turning off the gramophone, "Now it sounds just like my Dennis."

Andy didn't see Vera wince as she gazed at the gramophone. Vera handed him several shillings, "Our names, Nola and Vera, are sticky-taped on the side of our meters."

"You are kind," said Nola.

"Yes, kind," said Vera as Andy smiled, nodded, sneezed, wheezed, wiped away another handful of cold sweat and started down the stairs.

"They're lovely, them Yankee boys," added Vera as she sat by the dormant gas fire with a box of matches ready to welcome the return of heavenly warmth, "So polite, so gentlemanly in that tatty old bathrobe of his. Here! Haven't we seen that robe before, love?"

Nola lowered herself carefully into her chair, "It does look familiar doesn't it?"

"He looks poorly though, does our poor Yank, doesn't he?"

"It's that basement, isn't it?" said Nola, "Last one there died, didn't he?"

"Ummm," said Vera, "A paraffin fire was not forthcoming. A paraffin fire is definitely required at that depth."

"My Dennis has a paraffin fire, hasn't he? Two, in fact," said Nola.

"Well your Dennis lives in a basement doesn't he?"

"Vera! That was it! The Yank's bathrobe! It belonged to that poor, wasted, basement gentleman which died!" said Nola.

"And the gentleman before him, dear. I know this for a fact through the reprehensible Iris. It was a most unfortunate hand-me-down. Cursed. That basement is a menace to life," continued Vera with an exaggerated frown so that Nola, who was severely near-sighted, might more easily discern it.

"But we'd all of us be safer in a basement these days," said Nola, "We're for it now, aren't we, love? The Russian Peril. Them poor Yanks."

"We'll win, Nola, sooner or later. We always do."

"The bible says," said Nola, "and it must mean Russia, that 'The Great Black Bear from the North will sit astride this world."

"Not if he's got our knees, he won't!" snapped Vera.

"What a lovely boy," replied Nola, "his name is Leander."

"The Leander of Greek legend who, against great odds, swam the treacherous Hellespont time and again to be with his one true love, the high-priestess, Hero," recited Vera with some conviction and a far away glint in her eye.

"Staggering, Vera, that was simply staggering!"

"Only a school recitation, Nola. I was nine."

"Well, it's got my vote, dear."

Andy stood swaying on the next landing down. His head was now whirling and he felt sick, was certain the excessive drinking was, as Granddad would have put it, 'the chickens coming home to roost.'

He made it just in time to the toilet, slammed in and vomited. His night visitor's door cracked open, the head appeared and nodded sympathetically as its two bloodshot eyes squinted and suffered visibly with each noisy ejection into the toilet.

When he was finished, Andy returned to his room and dutifully inserted the shillings into the two ladies' meters.

He was just falling into bed as Iris, accompanied by Uncle's barking dogs and Uncle's curses, crashed into Andy's room with her rattling tray of breakfast. "Oh!" she said, seeing the untouched dish of potatoes and sprouts and ham, "Oh! Miss Pofford'll be ever so upset. You wasted her food!"

"I'm s-sorry. I was drunk. The w-welcome-wagon."

"Food don't grow on trees, as Miss Pofford says."

"Yes, it d-does," said Andy impatiently -- he was feeling wretched, even a little hysterical, "Apples d-do, oranges d-do, almonds d-d-do, avocados d-d-d-do and-and-and…you forgot to put m-money in Vera and Nola's…"

"No classes today?" said Iris, brushing away this incriminating comment and several of his drawings from the little table to make room for breakfast.

Andy coughed and said, "I'm s-sick."

"I'm not surprised," said Iris, "Living down 'ere in this damp where better men than you 'ave breathed their last. I wouldn't live here if my life depended on it!"

This struck Andy as funny and he laughed and immediately felt nauseated so he stopped. He agreed with Iris's 'better men than you' but had no idea what to do about it. It seemed he couldn't even draw now. Almost everybody was better than he was. With the possible exception of Marcella. He was terrified by this. His life needed work. But how important was his simple little life compared with the great catastrophe that awaited Humankind? He could not keep all this in proper balance. He coughed, found refuge in several more coughs as Iris grabbed up his untouched dinner and muttered "Miss Pofford'll be ever so upset," as she exited to renewed barking and swearing from Uncle's room. "Miss Pofford'd be ever so upset if she heard such cursing, Uncle," cried Iris from the hall.

"Stuff Pofford! And stuff you! Where's my breakfast?!"

"Soon, Uncle, dear" cried Iris, "Soon! We gave most of it to the Yank," she lied, "As he is poorly!"

"I-rees!" shrieked Miss Pofford, through the thinness, "I-rees!"

Andy's door was flung open, Iris rushed in, pressed her mouth to the crumbling, powdery thinness in the wall and shrieked:

"Coming, Miss Pofford!"

Andy sat in his bed wondering if Sheila was planning to be naked soon in this very same bed. Wondering what he would do if she tried. Wondering about Philippe -- what had happened? Nothing much, of course. Nothing that hadn't happened before. What's a little masturbation between friends? If there was a little masturbation. Although Philippe wasn't exactly a friend the French were certainly extremely friendly, generous, openhearted and accommodating. First a paraffin fire from Jean-Francois then the whisky and a wank, if it was a wank, from Philippe. 'A wank for a Yank' mused Andy who had, as dear Granddad might have remarked, a decided 'penchant' for said. Andy liked this new foreign word, 'wank', that seemed unavoidable here in England. He had heard it at least twice on the train to Oxford from his ship in Southampton and four times, including variations, at the Playhouse Bar during his one and only visit there on his one and only day at the Rossetti. He laughed again but he could not stop himself wondering why he was so nervous with Sheila and why it was so pleasant – whatever it was, if it was a wank with Philippe. The bourbon! That was it. Bourbon whisky was the solution to all unpleasantness in this disorganized, discourteous and dangerous world. Bourbon was the answer. But only if used wisely. In moderation. Alcohol could get out of hand. No. Bourbon was not the answer. He had no desire to bump into things, to fall and to bruise his elbows and knees and get big blue lumps on his head. To disappoint or frighten his future children. Then he began to worry about these children-to-be. How would he support them? What would their prospective mother think of him even if he wasn't an alcoholic? Who would their mother be? She'd end up hating him! Why did he ever get married?! Especially to her?

He wondered, too, if he'd ever be well enough to go back to the Rossetti, further wondered if he and the Rossetti would even be here tomorrow or the day after. This, of course, would put cancelled to his future wife and children. All that terrifying responsibility, up in smoke. But this was hardly comfort! His mind was a mess and President Kennedy was giving an important message tonight. Andy wondered what it would be. Then it suddenly occurred to him – and he was shocked by it -- that he hadn't thanked Irene and Jean-Francois for his paraffin fire. What in the world had happened to his manners?!

This was how great civilizations began their slow, inevitable declines, bit by discourteous bit. How they foundered. Things like not holding doors open for ladies, or escorting a blind person, maybe even the Blind Girl herself, across a street, or giving up ones seat on a bus to an old person or forgetting to say 'How very nice to have met you' when taking ones leave of a new acquaintance, particularly a more mature one. Forgetting these finer points of behaviour invited chaos. Chaos could lead anywhere. Absolutely anywhere! As it was now quickly proceeding to do in Cuba! Andy was frightened of 'anywhere.' He preferred 'somewhere.' Somewhere nice. Somewhere -- if possible -- cozy. And warm. Yes. Warm, please. Let it be warm again. But not too warm. But warmer, anyhow. Yes. Please!

JOAN AND JEAN ON PAGO-PAGO

She sat posture-perfect at the small, rattan dressing table glaring into its cracked mirror -- exactly as she had forty-five years before. Then, as now, it had rained continuously for one hellish week on this storm-ravaged little island, this tiny speck in the South Pacific where hot, tropical rain thundered just above her head on the low, tin roof and distant native drums warned of the recent arrival of plague. The pounding rain, a shattering bolt of lightning, and a tall glass of vodka had dramatically set the stage for a romp -- a romp with her frightening, illustrious past.

The woman rose from her bamboo chair, enjoying her graceful image in the mirror. She began to wander sedately around the shabby little rattan-bamboo hotel room, wary of memories she half-feared to tread upon. At a cheap, flowered dressing screen, she leaned over her open trunk, snatched out a mussed, black silk blouse, expertly folded it and laid it fussily back. She wandered on, remembering what had happened in the small mosquito-netted bed -- not a happy memory. On she went, circling, inspecting the little room. Precisely here was where she sat -- the chair was gone but she was certain she could see its imprint in the soft sea-grass matting. It was here she crouched as he read his sacred verses to her and she, desperate and disillusioned, had lapped them up, become a new woman, was glorified, cleansed, plucked free of sin.

The woman moved on. Here is where she fell as he threw down his holy book and pursued her. She imagined she could see the sea-grass matting that tore under her feet as she ran. Yes! Yes! There it was, unchanged! She had attempted escape through the double doors to a corner of the balcony -- where she cowered, and where he had taken her, brutally, as lightning flashed and jungle drums pounded, heightening the terror of the moment! It was the very essence of film drama! She closed her eyes, re-imagined not only her terror but how she rose above it, became more than that vile act itself. She defined, in that moment, a woman's terror. For all the world to see! The world saw and was astonished, terrified! The world was captivated! She had never let 'em down since!

This past-haunted woman resembled in no small way the classic American movie star, Joan Crawford, who had dazzled film-goers the world-over for forty years. Her face in that mirror, though it retained indelible traces of its former dark, stark beauty, had been coarsened by decades of cigarettes, cocktails, and the latter meddling of too many high-priced surgeons. Not to mention more than a few tall vodkas -- daily.

"I'm a goddamned knockout," announced Joan to her still arresting, still cinematically capable reflection in the mirror as she sat again. "Yeah," she muttered, through the comforting buzz of a vodka high, "I still got what it takes." She shot a suitably 'Joan' grimace at the mirror, quaffed the dregs of her glass, grabbed the bottle and one hand on hip poured another tall one, quaffed it, sighed relief and poured another. She studied herself for a moment, curled her mouth into a slatternly sneer, spat: "Nobody's gonna chase you outta Pago-Pago again! Are they, Sadie?" Then softer, "Are they, Lucille? Billie?" Softer still, "Are they...Joan?" She had intimately experienced all of these women. They were, of course, her. Was this the golden secret that had kept Joan Crawford those many years at the very pinnacle of stardom, this ever intriguing process of reliving her own kaleidoscopic life? Yes! shrieked a hundred fan magazines the world over.

Glistening tears appeared at the corners of both heavily mascaraed eyes and, on cue, her phrasing perfect, her tone ineffably tender, Joan whispered: "Are they, baby mine? Are they going to chase you out of Pago-Pago? *Again*?"

At this improbable moment, a rain-drenched woman in white, a small white case on one arm and a white leather bag on her shoulder, tottered on her highest of heels through torrents of hot rain, windswept waves of wet jungle grass, and the wild tangle of uprooted palms. This woman, who had presumably died of kidney failure in 1937 and resembled in no small way the legendary but short-lived 1930's film star, platinum blonde Jean Harlow, was stumbling through the furious storm toward the small ramshackle hotel wherein, at her bamboo dressing table, sat Joan Crawford, lately of immense Hollywood fame. Perhaps not so lately. It was already 1977.

Posture-perfect still, on her bamboo chair, Joan glared into her mirror mesmerized by her own famous face behind whose surprisingly smooth brow *the secret egg of a desperate plan would soon split and disgorge.* Joan loved that phrase -- she'd said it in one of her later horror films and it was splendidly apt for the occasion. But Joan and Jean were headed for a chronologically impossible collision and this was not in Joan's secret plan.

Bibulously unaware of the rapidly approaching Harlow, Joan set down her third -- or was it her sixth? -- vodka, grabbed a fine black handbag from the mildewed sea-grass matting at her feet and overturned it on the dressing table. A lipstick, compact, gold cigarette case and a tiny, shiny, pearl handled revolver clattered out. She took up the revolver, pressed it against her scarlet rouged cheek, gazed rapt, as her mirrored image smiled and silently reprised her strange, secret strategy.

Laying the tiny revolver aside, she took a cigarette from the cigarette case and lit it with a match -- someone, it seemed, had stolen her precious lighter. She inhaled, exhaled magnificently as only Joan Crawford could. Could and had, forty feet tall on a movie screen in innumerable films that rocketed her to ever greater stardom in the nineteen-thirties, forties and fifties.

Pago-Pago was the scene of the glittering triumph of her youth, the classic, "Rain". She had portrayed author Somerset Maugham's luckless prostitute, 'Sadie Thompson', filmed on this island. Filmed, much of it, here in this shabby little room.

Remembering had its revivifying advantages and Joan's eyes widened with rage, instantly darkened with pain, slowly moistened with heart-rending sorrow and segued into copious tears as memory pursued her from scene to scene revealing her broad, if startling, dramatic range. She had wowed them!

"Oh, yeah! I wowed the bastards!" shot Joan into her mirror and with the back of a much veined hand she swept away these copious tears so expertly summoned and quaffed another shot of vodka. But...Oh, Jesus! Her goddamned nose was red! What the hell?! Her face crumpled. She slumped, a ravaged rag doll in her bamboo chair, became again that island hopping, downhearted-doxy. "You were a triumph, sister! And you will be again!"

A last hopeful glance into the merciless mirror told her it was time now. It was time. The plan must proceed. Her rain and plague blighted visit to Pago-Pago would now become a sentimental journey with a terrifying twist! A plot to shock and draw the final curtain on her once colossal, but now much forgotten, career. People had such short, fucking memories. Sad, that. But true.

Now was the time. Joan's sudden, shattering demise by her own hand -- in Pago-Pago! -- would raise universal headlines and re-ignite the flaming torch of recognition for millions who had never heard of the great, late Joan Crawford! Her movies would be shown again and again! The tiny, pearl handled revolver at her elbow would facilitate this daring coup de théâtre. At the exact location of her greatest early triumph she would take her own life!

She took up the little revolver, smoothed it tenderly against her face once more. She had been told by an expert that to kill with so small a calibre, this revolver must be placed directly against the head -- or possibly up her nose -- or in her mouth. Yes, the mouth was the most reliably macabre. She would throw The World Press raw meat!

Her 1940's sculptured, red lips now parted to receive the gun's muzzle but a very loud knock at the door of her shabby little room caused her to frown. Another very loud knock caused her to growl. The hammering at her door grew louder. Crawford grunted irritably and casually applied thicker lipstick and tossed the tiny revolver back into her handbag. She splashed out another vodka and as the hammering at her door continued, stubbed out her cigarette and lit another and took a lazy puff. Glass in one hand, cigarette in the other, she crossed her shapely legs as provocatively as she had for John Garfield in the great film classic, 'Humoresque', struck a pose, shouted "Enter!"

The hammering immediately ceased and the door swung open. In an aura of white light, emanating it seemed, from the very purest soul, stood the twenty-six year old, platinum-haired woman. Even drenched she was impossibly gorgeous, impossibly luminous, in her sodden white chiffon, her huge, white but wilted picture hat and her white, impossibly high heels. It was indeed, though impossibly, Jean Harlow. She of that untimely death forty years before. It was this impossible Harlow, meltingly lovely, who now stared at Joan and after a long, wide-eyed and poignantly cinematic moment, spoke.

"Hey!" she exclaimed!"

Joan, irritated, stiffened and glared back at her.

"Hey!" said Jean again and set down her small white case. "Hey!" she repeated as she rapidly batted her abundant eyelashes and stared, awestruck at Joan and said yet again, "Hey!"

"Hay is for horses!" spat Joan.

"If the shoes fit, honey, wear 'em," grinned Jean, her timing perfect, as she took a compact and a lipstick from her shoulder bag. Bathed in Joan's glowering frown, she puckered, carefully applied lipstick, and inspected her luscious lips. Satisfied, she dropped the compact and lipstick into her bag and cried, "Hey! Weren't you Joan Crawford?!"

"*Am* Joan Crawford, and I didn't ring for the maid! So who the hell are you?!"

"Who d'you think, Joanie?"

Frowning, Joan took a swig from her glass and an elegant drag on her cigarette and exhaled magnificently. "This is 1977. Harlow died in '37. Forty years ago. This is not possible."

"Anything's possible, honey. Jeez, I never been so far from home before. Whaddaya call this place anyhow?"

"*My room*, darling," hissed Joan. "We call it *my* hotel room."

Jean rummaged through her bag, drew out a travel brochure and, reading, announced, "Pago something? Yeah, this place is called Pago..."

"Pago-Pago!" snapped Joan.

"Jeez! I heard ya the first time! And ya don't have to shout! Ain't you goin' to ask me in?"

"Why?" said Joan.

"Why not?" said Jean and smiled a mock-desperate smile, "I'm soakin' wet! And they lost my suitcase on the boat over."

Joan's nostrils flared significantly as she exhaled a silvery burst of smoke and with a sharp gesture of her cigarette, motioned in the dripping Jean. With an elaborate curtsy, Jean shot Joan an impish wink, swooped up her small, white case, a wind-up portable phonograph, sashayed into the room and dropped herself on the run-down sofa. Grinning, she carefully placed the phonograph by her feet and ripped off her rain-wilted picture hat, tossed it on the floor. Joan immediately sprang up to rescue the huge, wide-brimmed hat and shaped and carefully smoothed it and placed it on a table while puzzled Jean watched. This was a menial job, thought Jean, this was certainly a job for the wardrobe department. "You sure you're Crawford, honey?"

Joan stiffened as though struck in the face. "As sure as

you're little Miss Jeanie Harlot." Joan thought: She's drenched. Let her suffer for a while in this stinking room. I did.

Jean leaned back on the sofa, artfully arranging her glorious breasts against the sodden, white chiffon of her dress. A beautifully manicured finger flew to her chin as she peered at the uncomfortable Joan. "Watcha been doin' to yerself, Joanie, honey? Takin' granny-pills? My poor old Mama looks younger'n you."

Joan frowned, splashed out another vodka, downed it.

"So that's it!" squealed Jean, "You're a drinker! So we've both of us got a little problem. I'll tell you mine if you tell me yours!"

Joan held up a bottle of vodka and hissed, "Have a little drinkie."

Jean shook her head, pointed to a soda siphon on a nearby tray, stroked her cheeks, said "Somethin' soft, please, honey, for the skin men love to touch. And touch and touch. But you stick to the hard stuff, Joanie. No use lockin' the stable door after horsey's bolted!"

Jean's delicious laugh did not deter Joan from snatching up the soda siphon and aiming a hefty burst into Jean's lap. Jean sprang up and shook herself girlishly but only giggled as Joan riffled through her trunk and returned with a sheer kimono and a towel, tossed them on the sofa beside Jean. She poured another vodka and squirted a glassful of soda, sat on the sofa arm and handed the glass to Jean, who said, "'Sides, I'm a Christian Scientist jist like my Mama. I'm a teetotaler. I got principles, honey."

Joan choked on her drink but managed, "Now that we know my problem, Harlow, What's yours?"

"Our problem, Missy Crawford, big-time movie star, ma'am," said Jean as she expertly doffed her wet, white dress and underclothes, toweled herself and slipped naked into the kimono and sat. "Our problem," she continued kittenishly over the rim of her glass, "Is this here room..."

"*My* room!" snapped Joan.

"Your room, Miss Queen of Sheba, has been double booked."

"Impossible! I booked this room months ago for my...my..."

"Yeah?" said Jean, "Zat so?"

Joan's glass was shaking slightly, but not enough to splash her vodka. "I booked this special room four months ago for my goddamned sentimental journey. A double booking is impossible!"

"Not in good old Pago-Pago," sang the jovial, impossible Jean, "'Specially when they're havin' a hurricane, honey. 'Specially when there's a epidemic. 'Specially then."

Jean smoothed the sheer kimono lovingly to her luscious breasts, stood and wandered through the bamboo double doors to the tin-roofed balcony. The torrential rain grew louder and distant drums echoed ominously from the jungle.

"Jeez!" said Jean, "Don't it never stop?" She casually lifted her arm and pointed into the jungle as warm tropical wind tangled platinum curls framing her glowing face. "They're havin' a epidemic, Joanie! Out there!" declared Jean, as the concerned heroine of some long forgotten adventure film.

"Don't be dramatic," hissed Joan, "This isn't Hollywood."

"They're dyin' like flies out there, sister, and you better believe it!" insisted the radiant Jean.

Joan brought a hand to her ripe, red lips and, as though conscious of a fortuitously hidden camera, yawned a perfect cinema-yawn, said "Harlow, you sound like a character in a long, boring film."

Jean turned from the storm, faced Joan with a naughty grin. "You oughtta know, Joanie. You made enough of 'em."

"For chrissake, stop calling me Joanie!"

Jean shrugged, returned to lean against a large bamboo chair.

"And sit down!" cried Joan, You make me nervous!" But Joan thought: Are they really having an epidemic out there?

-- she was becoming so forgetful lately. It was worrying. She answered herself aloud: "Of course they are, Sadie, just like last time."

"Jeez," whispered Jean, "she talks to herself," but Jean sat, said, "You been here before?!"

"I made a movie here! 'Rain'. In 1932. That's why I'm here, isn't it? I'm on a goddamned sentimental journey because I made a goddamned movie here!"

Jean had just taken a swig of soda which now exploded. "Sweetie," she coughed and wiped her mouth with several pretty fingers, "Sweetie, you couldn't of."

Joan stiffened, "And why not?!"

"Because, Joanie, that movie ain't been made yet. Not the talkin' version anyhow. It ain't been made yet."

Joan shot up from the sofa, marched through the balcony doors, thrust out her arms, "Impossible!" she cried, posing impressively against the torrential jungle backdrop. "We made the movie here! I know every inch of this place! You're nuts!"

Jean did not wish to further offend Joan, so satisfied herself with an intimate whisper: "I better not tell her I'm here to replace her. She'd moider me!"

After an elaborate hand-wringing moment of perfectly edited contemplation on the balcony, Joan returned. "I don't know what the hell you're talking about! 'Rain' was made! Here! I was Sadie! Everyone says you're a crazy broad, Harlow..."

"Takes one to know one," giggled Jean and brushed a wet, platinum curl from her smooth, creamy white forehead.

"It is no secret, Harlow, that you screwed your way to fame and fortune on the fabulous silver screen."

"Now let's not get all sweaty and autobiographical, Joanie! It ain't becomin'!"

Jean waved her peaches and cream arms over her head, began to scream with laughter. She arched her back against the sofa and yet again forced her lovely breasts into a strategically promising camera angle. Where was the camera? She didn't know. Nor did Joan.

Joan was instantly threatened, wondered who this impossible and impossibly beautiful facsimile of Harlow could possibly be. But she remained silent and removed herself to the dressing table. With large fluid gestures and much turning of head she began to apply, yet again, her deep scarlet lipstick.

Jean was profoundly struck by Joan's tireless, movie-screen demeanour, watched her create the full, sumptuous mouth for which Crawford was world renowned. As Joan finished she turned to Jean, whose wide eyes could not conceal her admiration. Joan touched her lips, smiled ruefully and said, "These lips are what's known as a trademark. My trademark."

"What trade?" chirped Jean and began to giggle. Joan ignored her. She'd suffered far worse than the harmless chatter of this bleached blonde mediocrity.

Joan knew that Jean had been terrified of the makeup department at the Metro film studio. They had attempted to make Jean into something she wasn't, and could never be -- a film star of the magnitude of Joan herself. Jean's hair was naturally mousey-brown, not the luminous platinum blonde that lit the screen. Jean's lips were smaller than the vulgar lipstick contour they troweled on -- nothing like Joan's more than ample cupid's bow that, with one gorgeous grimace, could stun a man at ten paces.

Jean's difficulties, Joan was certain, weren't only in the makeup department. It was Wardrobe too -- those impossible clothes they'd forced the little slattern into and tried to teach her how to wear, or not to wear. She had no class. Christ! The skimpy blouses were invariably a mile off her shoulder and well into forbidden tittie territory. The lack of a bra must have allowed painful abrasion of Jean's nipples against the sheerest of materials, even the gentlest chiffon of her latest ensemble.

What had that to do with acting?!

"My Christ!" muttered Joan, "You are a simple slut!"

Joan swigged from her tall glass, took a sensational drag at her cigarette, exhaled equally as remarkably and studied Jean for a moment and said "But charming in a silly shop-girl sort of way. What's *your* trademark, Harlow?"

Jean was flattered that formidable Joan -- or whoever she was -- had cared enough to ask and she bubbled excitedly, "Everybody says it's my hair but it's really my bazooms! Most always, you can see my cute little nipples through the various fabrics!" Jean pulled the kimono tight across her breasts. "See?"

Joan puffed idly at her cigarette and gazed sphinx-like at Jean who mimed dialing a telephone and whispered into it. "Know what I'm doin', Joanie?"

Joan frowned and rolled her eyes.

"I'm whisperin' sweet nothin's into my own ear. Makes my nipples go hard and stand right up. They photograph good, Joanie." Jean grinned like an old friend, approachable, intimate; a look she had perfected on the screen -- the gorgeous, good-time gal.

"Know what I'm sayin', Joanie?"

"Nix with the 'Joanie', Harlow."

"I am sayin' Hi there, pretty little nipples, stand up and smile for the camera!"

Joan turned away in disgust. Jean giggled and snuggled back in her chair but rose suddenly, and ambled through the double doors to the balcony again. There she stood and nobly stuck out her chin as she had just minutes before, as had the heroine in her last film. That was merely a rehearsal, this was the real thing -- but where was the darned camera?! She batted her unmissable eyelashes and gravely gestured toward the tragedy she knew to be unfolding just across the jungle. The native drums grew louder, as on cue, and she cried "They're dyin' like flies out there, Joanie. Us movie stars gotta do somethin' about it!"

"Oh, give it a rest! We're sharing a goddamned room!" snapped Joan, "what more do they want?!"

Jean sauntered back and sat beside Joan, said "Then I can stay?"

"Lovey," said Joan softly, "I never said you couldn't." She took Jean's hand, "Did I?"

Jean deftly removed her hand, said "I'm hungry."

"Who isn't?" said Joan and again took Jean's hand. Jean again withdrew and yelled "Jiggers! Duh cops!" as someone pounded on their rickety rattan door.

"Who is it?" inquired Joan at her steely best.

"Dinner, Missies," said the Filipino cook. I set by door. Me no come near."

"Missies?!" giggled Jean.

"Hush! Harlow!" Then, to the door. "Was our food prepared with face masks and rubber gloves?"

"Me no understand, Missy," said the cook.

"Did you wash your hands?" demanded Joan.

"Missy, me no speakee --"

"Our food!" cried Joan, "Was it prepared under strictly hygienic conditions?!"

"Me no speakee the English, Missy."

"We do not wish to be infected! Your epidemic --" continued Joan.

"Me no speakee, Missy. Me go now."

"Come back here, you septic bastard! You are not dismissed!" cried Joan and turned to Jean. "Our food may be dangerously infected."

Jean shrugged. Joan suspiciously surveyed her, hissed, "Did anyone touch you? How did you get here?"

"Joanie, we are on a island. I sure as Hell didn't come on the back of a elephant."

"Did you have intimate contact with the natives?!" spat Joan.

Jean laughed. "You been seein' too many of yer own movies,

Joanie."

Joan rose from the dressing table and began to pace. She swept back and forth across the squeaking, sea-grass matting, pausing after each traverse to scowl for a camera close-up on the forty-foot movie screen that was nowhere to be seen.

Jean, though deeply fascinated with Joan's extravagant emoting, was hungry and went to the door, opened it. Joan backed away much as a devil might if God walked in the room. It was an old tried and true shtick she'd used in this very room forty-five years before and was applauded for it by the film crew.

Jean brought in a large dinner tray, set it carefully on a rattan table and lifted a cover from one of the dishes. She bent over it, sniffed and sighed with pleasure. "My tummy's grumbling! Yummy, yummy! Somethin' for my tummy!"

Joan kept a safe distance as Jean sat grinning, and twirled a fork high in the air -- a trick of hers for which her filming crew also applauded. But then, the crew applauded all her scenes, especially the ones with nipples.

"Come on over, Joanie, and chow down. You don't know what yer missin'! Yum-yum!" called Jean, and began, pseudo-erotically, to eat. She sighed after each sumptuous bite, and glanced covertly at Joan who crept slowly, meaningfully, in for a closer look at both Jean and the food, then hovered nearby, dragging elegantly on her cigarette.

"Dive in, honey!" cried Jean affectionately. "The water's jist fine!"

Joan turned suddenly, marched to her trunk and returned with a spray-can of disinfectant, grabbed one of the dishes, lifted its cover and daintily sprayed it. She took a bite and made a grim face.

Jean, chewing, stared opened-mouthed at her.

"Close your mouth when you chew, Harlow. Didn't Hollywood teach you anything?"

Jean smiled to herself as she watched Joan grimacing over

each disinfected bite of her suspicious food.

"I was wonderin', Joanie..."

"For God's sake, finish chewing your food before you speak!"

Jean gulped down her mouthful. "I was jist wonderin', Joanie --"

"Everyone who matters, calls me *Joan!*"

"Among other things," murmured Jean under her breath, then, "I was wonderin', *Joanie*. They lost my luggage and I was wonderin' if you had anything I could wear. Like underwear."

"Underwear? Don't you mean *lingerie*?"

"Whatever you say, Joanie," grinned Jean, "panties, bra, condoms?"

Joan registered wide-screen disapproval, "Condoms?!"

"Come on, honey, you jist gotta know about condoms. You must go through enough condoms in a week to build a trampoline!" Jean laughed. "'Cause if you didn't, you'd be the mother of us all!"

Jean, laughed raucously, choked on her food.

"But Missy Harlow doesn't wear lingerie," countered Joan, arched eyebrow at least twenty feet tall.

"Don't believe everything you read, Joanie. It's dangerous."

"Dangerous?" snapped Joan, "Like murdered husbands?"

Jean went pale, dropped her fork.

"Did you or did you not murder your husband, Harlow?"

"It was just like the papers said. Suicide, I tell ya!"

"Ah!" said Joan, "Then we *should* believe everything we read?"

"Yeah, honey, believe it." Jean unscrewed the salt shaker, emptied it over Joan's food. "But take it with a grain of salt."

Joan, to Jean's horror, snatched up her fork and continued to eat her salt-laden, spray-can disinfected food and announced, "Discipline, darling. Discipline!"

Jean could bear it no longer and pushed Joan's dish away from her.

"You couldn't eat this, could you?" snapped Joan, "Not if your tiny phony-blonde life depended upon it."

Jean shook her head.

"I could eat shit if I had to. To stay alive," said Joan. It tastes like everything else on the menu. There are worse things in Hollywood than eating shit."

Jean began suddenly to giggle. Joan ignored her.

"Sorry, Joanie," she said. "All of this poop talk reminds me of a joke my Auntie Graycie told me. May I?"

"If you must."

Jean flashed a fabulous smile, arched her back provocatively, accentuating yet again those breasts men apparently loved to touch and touch and touch. She pushed herself away from her tray of food, giggled as she recalled the story, and began it:

"My Auntie Graycie was postmaster of this little old post office out in the hills somewhere in West Virginia." Jean paused, began to giggle.

"Get on with it!" said Joan, "Forgot your lines again?!"

"No, honey, I ain't." Jean brushed back her platinum locks and continued seriously:

"This old hillbilly which lived in a hermit cave way, way up in those hills came down to the post office once a month, ya see, to get his mail. You know, Joanie, his girlie magazines in plain brown envelopes?"

Jean giggled again, stretched idly and crossed her legs. "And every month when he came into her post office my Auntie Graycie would ask him, 'What's new, Lemuel?' For that was his name. And he would always shake his grizzled old head and he wouldn't say nothin'."

Joan rolled her eyes, found instant solace in a large swallow of vodka.

"But after Lemuel didn't come into the post office for about three months everybody got real worried that he mighta up and died out there in his dirty old cave and was just layin' there rottin' and stinkin'. And folks was thinkin' about sendin' for the sheriff...or somethin'."

"Or somethin'," muttered Joan and rolled her eyes and yawned.

"Well, he up and shows up one day. And my Auntie Graycie, she asks him --"

"What's new, Lemuel?" mumbled Joan, who gave a small snort and pretended to nod sleepily.

"Yeah, that's jist what she asked him. What's new, Lemuel? And you know what he said?"

Joan stared empty-eyed at Jean, took a large, lazy swallow from her tall glass, said, "Do tell, Jeanie, what the old geezer said. I'm jist a-dyin' of suss-pense."

"Well, Lemuel says..." Jean went into an even deeper hillbilly accent:

"He says...'I had a little dream t'other night, I did. I dreamed I was a horse, I did. And some mean bastard tied me to a post, he did. And he beat me. And he beat me. And I neighed and whinnied and pawed the ground with my horse's hoofs. And I commenced to shit. And I shat. And I shat. And I pawed and neighed and whinnied and shat and pawed and shat and pawed and shat and shat and shat some more!' Then this old timer looked real thoughtful and he chewed on his tobbaccy for a minute. Then he spit out his tobaccy into my Auntie Graycie's antique spittoon and he said: 'And do you know *what*, Miss Graycie?'

'No, Lemuel,' said my Aunt Graycie, as curious as all get-out, 'What?'

'Well,' said Lemuel, 'The next mornin' when I waked up, I really *had* shat!'"

Joan began to laugh. This was her kind of story. Jean was pleased and, laughing, they fell into one another's arms.

They continued to fall about giggling until Joan suddenly straightened up. Deadly serious, she lit a cigarette. "Now," she said, "Little Miss Jeanie Harlow, as they don't sell peroxide in fifty gallon vats in Pago-Pago, why have you come?"

"Why, to make a movie, Joanie, honey. I thought you knew. They sure should of told you."

"A movie? What movie?"

"Oh, come on, Joanie!"

"Who the Hell are you? Really?"

"I'm Jeanie, Joanie."

"Little Miss Harlot? Impossible! What movie did you come here to make?!"

"Don't tell me they didn't tell you. They must of told you. I'm replacing you as Sadie Thompson. In 'Rain'. I'm the new Sadie."

Joan stood, drew herself up. Lightning flashed, thunder crashed and the rain increased to a deafening din.

"You are replacing *me*?" hissed Joan, her face a forty-foot tower of wrath.

"Gosh, I'm sorry, Joanie. They just needed a dame more... well, more supple, didn't they? Not so...angular, like. They just needed a dame more...well, like in ancient Greece, you know. Like in Helen of Troy."

"Helen of Troy?!"

"Yeah, honey. Kinda like in *legendary*."

"Legendary Helen of fucking Troy?!"

Joan took a long drag on her cigarette, a large swallow from her tall drink and strode to the very center of the little room. The rain beat down in great torrents. Lightning flashed again and thunder crashed again and the beat of ominous plague drums rose in the whistling wind -- all precisely on cue as Joan flung out her arms, faced the black roiling sky and shouted: "I HAVE *SUNK* MORE SHIPS THAN HELEN LAUNCHED!"

Unimpressed, Jean smiled tolerantly, tossed her platinum curls and took a compact from her bag, began to apply lipstick. "Well, honey, that's the whole point, ain't it? We wanna launch them ships not sink 'em!"

Jean held her little mirror away from her face, peered at the effect and dabbed a touch of powder on her very slightly shiny nose, nodded approval and giggled, "I'll have that little drinkie now, Joanie. Just a short one. I only drink to *ac*-cess."

Joan, expressionless, poured a glass for Jean, said "How are those kidneys of yours, Jeanie? If there's two things alcohol loves to hate, it's weak kidneys. We've heard stories, dearie, that your kidney twins are on their last wobbly legs. Make us happy, Harlot. Say it ain't so." Joan quaffed her tall vodka and sat as Jean daintily raised her own glass in a toast. "Here's to temperance, Joanie. Everything in moderation."

"Everything apparently, except murder," said Joan. "The murder of a loving husband. I don't trust platinum-blondes. Especially if they're widows. I could have married that film producer bastard of yours. He asked me often enough. Poor Jeanie. Everyone but you knew something was up. Or rather..." Joan leered, "*wasn't* up."

"So what?" said Jean. "So he wasn't horizontally upward-mobile. Everything don't depend on sex, Joanie. Big deal. He was a kind, intelligent man."

"He was a sadist!"

"He was a gentleman!" cried Jean.

"A gentleman? A gentleman?! In Hollywood..." snapped Joan, savagely stubbing-out her cigarette in a coconut shaped ashtray, "...a gentleman in Hollywood is only a jerk who removes the dishes before he pisses in your kitchen sink!"

Joan lit another cigarette, brutally puffed it to life. "You just married him to goose up your career. You were fizzlin' out, Harlow. You're the kind of broad who takes shortcuts. I'm the kind who works my ass off."

Jean, her gaze naughtily shifting to Joan's posterior, said "Well, honey, that ain't what it looks like from here."

"Oh, how I watched you at Metro," said Joan, "Everything came so easily to you didn't it? You never even bothered to learn to act. You just dyed your mousey hair platinum, closed your eyes and poked out your titties and caught the first poor producer-fish who nibbled at 'em. But after you'd hooked him and hoisted him in, you found he wasn't such a big fish after all! He wasn't a shark among men, was he, Jeanie? He was a goddamned guppie."

"Leave him alone! He ain't even cold in his grave!" cried Jean.

"Yet little Miss Jeanie Harlow trotted right over to Pago-Pago to make movies and didn't even bring along her widow's weeds."

"They're in my suitcase, I tell ya! It got lost. I'd changed into something cooler. I was hot!"

"After that sexless marriage, I'm not surprised."

"I've heard stories about you, Crawford. I wouldn't believe them. Couldn't believe them! Orgies..."

"I like sex and sex likes me," said Joan.

"If I was you, Joanie, I'd stay away from liquor and men. 'Cause somethin' ain't treatin' you right."

Joan rose, strutted about, gesturing broadly as she spoke.

"When Clark Gable kissed me I thought: If he lets me go now, I'll fall flat on my ass. We were lovers, Clark and I. For years. It was our monumental secret. We were the only people to whom we could speak the truth. We were the salt of the fucking earth."

"I thought you looked a little dusty, Crawford. Jeez! You could lose a lipstick in them creases around your mouth. I ain't surprised you lay it on with a garden spade."

"Clark was special. Other men weren't," said Joan and draped herself against the balcony doorway. Ignoring Jean, she stared into the hot, pouring rain. "Other men were like new dresses. I had to try them on to see if they fit. I would drive at night in my ice-blue Cadillac convertible along the silvery rim of the great Pacific Ocean. Pacific, as defined in Webster's dictionary, means *of a peaceful disposition*. It does not apply to me."

Joan laughed and strolled elegantly to the balcony. "With the wind in my hair and lots of money, I would speed along till I saw a pleasant prospect and I'm not talking about the landscape, sister. I'd screech to a stop beside tall, dark and whomever and I'd say: Hop on, stranger. And I meant it."

"I feel dirty," sighed Jean, "I need a bath."

"They couldn't say no to me," said Joan. "That is power. Star power. I never waited for things to happen. I made things happen. I still make things happen."

"I need a bath, I tell ya!"

"I wouldn't trust the water in this dump," spat Joan.

Jean brushed past Joan to the balcony, held her hand into a small torrent of hot rain. "Hey, Joanie! there's this special hole in the roof and a wooden tub just underneath it! Ain't I the lucky one?!" Jean dipped her hand into the tub water. "It's warm and clean. Pure rainwater."

"Enchanting," sniffed Joan as she carefully appraised Jean who had slipped out of the kimono and stood gloriously nude in yet another flash of perfectly timed lightning.

"Got a towel, honey?" grinned Jean into Joan's envious, dark eyes.

Joan tore her gaze from Jean's sensational breasts and left the balcony to return with the largest white towel Jean had ever seen, tossed it to her, and said "Compliments of the house."

"Oh!" chirped Jean, and giggled, "I didn't know we was in a 'House', honey!"

Jean flung the towel on a hook and wandered naked amidst the fragrant tropical flowers that cascaded over the balcony. She stood, stretched languidly into the narrow hot, torrent that had filled the wooden tub, sighed as rain flooded over and trickled in warm rivulets from her full, firm breasts.

Jean was enjoying every second of Joan's undisguised perusal of her nubile flesh. She had heard stories of Joan's multi-sexuality and had no reason to doubt them as she boldly posed, leaving nothing to Joan's imagination. At last she climbed lazily into the wooden tub of warm rain water, squealed delightedly and called "Got any soap, honey?!"

Joan hurried away and returned with a small, ornate bar of soap and a packet of bubble-bath powder. She tossed the soap to Jean who caught it smartly and flashed a fabulous movie-grin of thanks. Joan ripped open the packet of bubble-bath and sprinkled it into the grateful Jean's tub, then, drink in one hand, cigarette in the other, Joan sat on a crude bamboo bench peering lovingly at Jean.

Jean merrily splashed the bubble bath into a foam and lazily washed the back of her neck with the small bar of soap and attempted to appear just as she had when bathing in a barrel in the film 'Red Dust' with Clark Gable. "Oh!" she giggled, "Don't I jist smell gorgeous!"

"Nice soap, isn't it?" said Joan. "I have it flown in from Paris, France."

"Yeah, it's gorgeous! what's it called?"

"Pussy Willing!"

"S'nice," giggled Jean, "Jeez, is it always rainin' in this burg? It's been rainin' since the minute I stepped off the boat. It's creepy," whimpered Jean.

"Creepy," agreed the new, now genial Joan.

Ravishing, and utterly relaxed, Jean lay back in the water, sighed three sighs, each perfectly synched to three delicious grins and the suitable batting of those magnificent eyelashes.

As Jean luxuriated in her rustic bubble bath, Joan watched eagerly and vainly attempted to understand why everything came so easily to this golden young woman while she, Joan, the wholly artificial creation of herself and the Metro studio, had to fight every inch of her way up that *glittering ladder of success*.

"*I* bathed here too," said Joan defensively, "In that very tub, when I was about as old as you are now. How old are you, Jean?"

"Twenty-something, Joanie. How old are you?"

"I'm ageless."

"Feelin' your agelessness, honey? It's about time, ain't it? Wheeee!" splashed Jean, "I just love bubbles 'n' soap!"

"Apply the soap in light, upward strokes or you'll dry your skin," cautioned Joan, sincerely, to some unseen camera.

"Our face is our fortune, ain't it?" replied Jean, looking deeply into Joan's eyes. "Or *was* your fortune, Joanie. Maybe you ain't feelin' quite so fortunate anymore?"

Nothing Jean said could now make Joan take offense at this girl's callous remarks. "The young are cruel," murmured Joan, "especially in Hollywood. I know I was. Besides..." and she smiled, "this poor young woman has been dead for forty fucking years."

Jean, splashed and grinned happily at Joan.

"Be kind to your face, dear," said Joan softly, "and it will be kind to you."

"Seems like you could do with a little kindness," giggled Jean.

"I was a triumph as Sadie Thompson," replied Joan.

"Sure, honey. If you say so."

"It was tough playing a whore," said Joan.

"My dear hubby, Paul, the lord rest his immortal soul, told me that a actress draws on her own personal experience in life," said Jean. "Whether she knows it or not. Should of been easy then, Joanie, shouldn't it of? Playin' that whore?"

"Whaddaya mean by that?" snapped Joan, suddenly roused from her romantic torpor.

"My poor old Paul said know thyself!"

"What else was your dead would-be film producer husband besides an impotent encyclopedia?"

"My hubby had a lotta brains!" cried Jean.

"Then why did he blow them out with his pistol?"

"Then you admit it was suicide and that I didn't moider him?" said Jean.

"I'll give you the benefit of a doubt, for now, Miss Jeanie." Joan took a long drag on her cigarette, shuddered, said "Yeah, I know he had a lot of brains. He was sensitive too. Like me. I carry a revolver myself. In my bag. For protection. So no one can take...liberties."

"Ain't liberty no fun no more, Joanie? Ain't it a free country?"

"Too many Hollywood parties," sighed Joan. "God! I'd spend days preparing myself. Finding the right dress, fur, shoes, jewelry, makeup. I'd have a dee-licious sauna and a steam, a massage so I'd be super supple. I'd have my body anointed with oil and sponged off..."

"Ummmnnn," said Jean. "Know whatcha mean!"

"Do you?"

"Sure, honey. Parties always make me sweat a lot. Turns my darned ermines yellow under the arms."

Joan rolled her eyes, took a deep drag on her cigarette and continued fervently, "At the appointed hour I'd show up and make my grand entrance from the studio limousine. I was a goddamned knockout. My skin glistened, my hair shone, my eyes were bright as searchlights. The crowd parted..."

"Maybe you blinded 'em, honey, with them searchlights, huh?" said Jean.

"Do you know, Harlow, how to get your eyes bright as searchlights? No. Of course you don't. Because it's got to come from deep in here!" Joan slammed her chest, coughed on her cigarette.

"Forget the searchlights, Joanie. I just stick out my titties and go straight ahead and I ain't been stopped yet."

"Lovey," said Joan, "You'll rinse away like soap and nobody will ever know you existed. You'll be a greasy ring around that dirty wooden tub."

"That ain't what a hundred million Americans say!"

"A hundred million Americans ain't me! I am Joan Crawford and don't you ever forget it because nobody else will! I've seen to that! I'm immortal!"

"I don't mean to shock you or nothin', honey. But in fifty years all your gonna be is a big old pile of stale lipsticks and mouldy shoulder pads."

"You've got to concentrate to make your eyes as bright as searchlights!" cried Joan.

"Jesus, Joanie! Leave off with the searchlights! Who wants to make their darned eyes look like searchlights?!"

"I do! That's who!"

"What are you, honey, the night train to cuckoo-land?!"

"I loved those parties," said Joan. "Women gasped at the perfection of my clothes and my ice-cold demeanour." She dragged thoughtfully at her cigarette. "Men were forced to sit to hide their rising lust. Drink in one hand, cigarette in the other and every eye upon me, I'd move from one opulent room to the next..."

"Lightin' the way with them big old searchlight eyes of yours, huh?"

"I was the queen of all I surveyed. I was sublimely unapproachable."

"That ain't what I heard," giggled Jean.

"Shut up!" Joan drained her glass, poured another. "As it grew late, things always hotted up. I'd usually wander upstairs to the various powder rooms..."

"Checkin' out the action, huh?" Jean's eyes gleamed.

"They wouldn't even bother to lock their doors."

"The more the merrier, huh?" Jean lifted a lovely leg in the air, soaped her shapely foot.

"One could witness every conceivable sexual act and some I had thought not possible," said Joan.

"Woo-woo!" giggled Jean and playfully splashed the sudsy rainwater in her wooden tub.

"Toward the end. I mean at the time I stopped going to these parties, I could only look at these rooms upon rooms of sweating, tangled, aroused flesh and think..." Joan paused.

"Yeah, honey? I'm listenin'." Jean was avid, eyes shut,

scrubbing softly again at back of her neck. "Of what could you only think of, honey?"

"I could only think: Who in this crummy joint do I have to screw to get a kiss?"

"With me it's the other way around," added Jean, grinning.

"I thought it might be, mused Joan."

Rising like Venus from the wooden tub, Jean reached for the towel but Joan was instantly there, held it up for her and wrapped it round her and dried her lovingly. Joan knew that she must never again attempt to compete with Jean's cheap, youthful magnetism. Cheap or not, it had attracted Joan herself. Youth and beauty, Joan knew, would forever trump her elderly elegance, hypnotic face or most perfect shtick and she began to suffer in a grandly cinematic way. She might have used this in her next movie. But there was to be no next movie.

"Got a ciggie, Joanie?"

Jean wrapped herself in Joan's magnificent bath-towel, sat on the bamboo bench and watched avidly as Joan pulled two cigarettes from her gold case and placed both modishly between her lips. She lit them with a match, puffed them to life, and slipped one between Jean's lips. Precisely as had Paul Henreid, for Bette Davis in 'Now, Voyager'.

The women took a puff.

"All I ever wanted from life was a little affection," sighed Joan, "Just a little goddamned tender affection."

"I know whatcha mean, Joanie. It's lonely way up here at the top, ain't it?"

"Yeah, baby, the air is thin at the top," sighed Joan and took a long drag at her cigarette. "So now when the bastards try to use me I --"

"But what about all them drives along the blue Pacific, honey, in yer icy-blue caddy convertible? Pickin' up fellas right and left?"

"Don't you see the difference?" cried Joan. "They weren't

using me. I was using them. That goes for husbands too. When I had them where I wanted them I didn't want 'em anymore."

"What about all that tender affection stuff you was always searchin' for?" whispered Jean.

"It doesn't live in Hollywood. It never did. I had no time to change the world."

"So you just got old," said Jean, safely ensconced in her eternal, voluptuous youth.

Joan bowed her head then lifted her face beseechingly, to the sky, exactly as she had in innumerable strong-women roles. "It does seems so," she said softly, and jumped up, rushed back to her handbag and drew out the tiny pearl handled revolver. She returned and aimed it out over the balcony. "Now nobody messes with Billy Cassin. That's me! Lucille-LeSueur-Billy-Cassin and Ms Joan Crawford! They're all *me*, baby!"

"I can surely see why you shortened it, honey. They could of never of got it onto a movie marquee," said Jean and ignored the tiny revolver and toweled away at her wet hair.

"My mother was a nagging bitch!" said Joan, toying with the revolver.

"Mine was a Christian Scientist," sighed Jean. "But I never learned much about it."

"Why?" asked Joan.

"Cause I could never pry Mama out from underneath of my stepfather long enough to get a straight answer about anything."

The two women laughed, gazed fondly at one another.

"My mother hounded and beat me," said Joan as Jean tied the huge towel around herself and casually began to pick exotic flowers from the wind-tumbled vines. She placed the flowers in her hair and between her breasts at the edge of her towel.

"When I'd had enough," said Joan, "I ran away."

"Enough is enough, ain't it, honey? Good for you!"

Joan plucked one of the flowers from between Jean's breasts, toyed with it as she spoke. "I hit the road with a vaudeville troupe. I was one hot dancer."

"Jeez!" Jean paused to inspect an imaginary blemish on her shoulder. "Jeez, how inneresting!"

"I was knocked from pillar to post and back again," said Joan. "I ended up as a dance hostess in a ballroom where jerks bought tickets to pinch my ass and then some." She tucked Jean's flower behind her ear and aimed the revolver out over the balcony again, cried "Bang! Bang!" and lowered the gun, "All before I was eighteen."

"Jeez, you poor kid. I was only a Christian Scientist. Mama seen to that."

"But she let you die, didn't she?"

"Huh?"

"At twenty-six," said Joan. "At twenty-six your kidneys gave out after that sunlamp sunburn. Your Mama wouldn't let a doctor near you. You'd better come in now. You'll get a chill."

"But I ain't cold," protested Jean snatching another large blossom and tucking it into her towel.

"Let's go inside," said Joan, "The rain is beginning to blow in. Mama says let's go inside!"

"Okay. When you put it that way, Joanie. But could you stow that pearl handled gat, huh? They go off sometimes," said Jean, and followed Joan back into the shabby room where Joan laid her revolver on the dressing table and said in her faux-motherly way, "You used too much soap, darling. You'll look like a crocodile."

"Look who's talkin'. Got any *lingerie?*"

Joan disappeared behind the flowery bamboo screen, returned with white lace panties and a bra and handed them to Jean who immediately said, "The bra's too small."

"Like hell it is!" snapped Joan.

"Jeez! Look! I even took out your falsies and yer bra's still too small."

"My, my! What shall we do?! Tie your boobs down with a couple of beach umbrellas?!"

"And the butt's too big in the panties!" said Jean. "I thought you had a narrow butt, Crawford. It looks like that in the movies. Adrian musta stuffed ten or twenty shoulder-pads into them wide shoulders he designed for you, so's folks wouldn't notice that you're broad across your butt. Jeez, honey, with them hips you coulda borned a baby hippopotamus!"

"Give me back my lingerie!" screamed Joan.

"Sure, Joanie, if you say so."

Joan snatched her underwear away and returned, calmer, with a lovely, sheer, white negligee.

"That's more like it," said Jean. She pulled on the negligee and looked *simply delectable*, as the Fan-Mags had put it time and again -- and she sashayed provocatively from lamp to lamp, flicking them on and throwing the darkening room into golden light and purple shadow. Perfect, she felt, for her peaches and cream complexion.

"What the hell do you think you're doing?! This is *my* hotel room!" screamed Joan. "I'll do the goddamned lighting if you please! Did you hear that, Harlow?! Get out of my life!"

Jean was now confidently winding up her phonograph. She ignored Joan, took a record from her large, stylish handbag, Placed it lovingly on the turntable and set on the tone arm. A low-down, jazz band began to play. Jean made a few exquisitely erotic turns to the music as Joan hovered, emoting conspicuously amongst the purple shadows. Smoking and drinking and muttering, she remained perfectly in sync with the forty-foot movie image in her head. "You never made a decent picture in your whole goddamned life!" shouted Joan at Jean who had continued to slow-dance with herself and who calmly answered without breaking rhythm, "I did so."

"Name one!"

"I done real good movies with Jimmy Cagney and Spencer Tracey and Cary Grant!"

"And you slept with every producer in Hollywood to get to do 'em!" cried Joan.

"So did you! And I done three movies with your Mr smarty-farty Clark Gable!"

"Don't you dare take that dear man's name in vain! Clark told me he carried you! Did you hear me, Harlow?! Clark said he made himself look bad in 'Red Dust' so you would look good! I never allowed an actor to do that in my life! Do you hear?! In my whole goddamned life!"

After a moment, an image of her own young self glimmered in Joan's head as she began to move to this same low, slow jazz she had danced to forty-five years before. As she swayed to the wail of a sad, blues trumpet, she watched, and ached, as Jean slow-shimmied ever more erotically. No one in their right mind, thought Joan, would be watching Joan Crawford now. Not while Jean Harlow shimmied her right off the silver screen.

"Clark Gable told me, told me personally that he carried you!" cried the suitably desperate Joan, wary that this altered lighting favored her much younger interloper -- this feckless actress who seemed somehow to have usurped her treasured pin-spot, Joan's personal spotlight, crucial to any reigning superstar's survival on the movie screen.

"Yeah. He carried me alright," stage-whispered gorgeous Jean. "He carried me from the set to his dressing room to his bed. We didn't get no sleep that night, neither."

Joan moved menacingly toward Jean who giggled and bounded away laughing, her negligee revealingly aflutter. Joan shut off the phonograph and slammed it shut. "You're a liar, Harlow! Clark Gable wouldn't have touched a lowlife like you with a ten foot pole!"

Jean giggled and threw herself on the sofa and kicked her feet into the air to keep fierce Joan at bay, giggled "Gable didn't need no pole, Joanie! He brung his own!"

"He did not!"

"Maybe he did and maybe he didn't but you can put this in yer pipe and smoke it, Miss high-falutin' Crawford! Nobody carries Jean Harlow. 'Cause I am a actress!"

Joan began to laugh.

"And *you* ain't," said Jean. "My poor hubby, Paul told me Miss Joan Crawford couldn't act her way out of a wet, paper bag! Bette Davis put you to shame! And them was his exact words!"

"I won a goddamned Oscar!"

"You never!" cried Jean.

"I did, about ten years after you kicked the bucket," said Joan and took a cigarette from her case and lit it with her usual aplomb. She took a bible from the dressing table drawer, strolled lazily to the balcony door and posed. She had changed her mind. She *would* retain her sacred preeminence on the silver screen -- who needed superficial beauty? She had the immense cunning of a long, sensational career. Who ever said shtick didn't matter? She would fear this cheap tart no more. Thrusting up her prominent chin, Joan stared into the rain. It was dark except for occasional lightning. The jungle drums came up on cue and the rain pounded in blustery bursts and Joan gloried in it as her confidence flooded back.

Jean studied Joan yet again. It was impossible to ignore the glitzy indolence with which she moved, her offhand poise as she lit and held and puffed her cigarette. Joan leant provocatively against the door. She was now the grinning prostitute, Sadie Thompson.

The light in the room shrank to a pin-spot on Joan's face and grateful for her beloved little spotlight's return, she spun from the balcony and thrust that bible into the air, shot Jean a slatternly leer, announced "I'm Sadie Thompson, see? I'm a lady of pleasure and I come to this broken down little island in the South Pacific and there's this epidemic goin' on and I can't get away and --"

"I know the story, Joanie," sighed Jean, who had draped

herself, in her stunning white negligee, over the sagging sofa.

"Shut up, Harlow! Listen and you'll learn something. Like maybe how to improve your totally non-existent technique, huh?"

Jean nodded reluctantly. Was this woman real?

"So, here I am!" said Joan, "I'm this prostitute and I get stuck in Pago-Pago in this crappy little bamboo hotel with this hellfire and brimstone, missionary preacher who's as loony as a long night in Alaska. But this crazy bastard thinks I'm a bad influence on the natives and tries to drive me outta Pago-Pago. Jesus! I didn't wanna be here in the first place, did I?! I'm stuck here, ain't I? On account of the weather and the plague! And the goddamned rain is drivin' me outta my fuckin' mind! Then the nutty sonofabitch decides he's gonna save me from Hell. So he converts me, see?" Joan held up the bible. "With this very bible. So I march around for a few hours in a plain cotton dress without no makeup, tearin' out my hair and gazin' up at heaven like I was waitin' for St. Peter to send the studio limou. Then this crazy preacher bastard decides he'd rather have my pussy than his pulpit and he rapes me. He's got to, see? 'Cause I won't dish out the goodies no more 'cause I'm converted, see? Then the sanctimonious asshole goes off and blows his brains out 'cause he's disappointed in hisself!" Joan grabbed the revolver from the table. "Blows 'em out with this very gun!"

Jean gasped. Joan dropped the gun on a table, the pin-spot disappeared and the lights came up somewhat, somehow.

"He may be a man of God, Harlow, but he's like all the rest. Men want one thing from a woman, honey, and don't you never forget it!" Joan smiled maniacally. "But God put Joan Crawford on this earth to make goddamn sure the horny bastards don't always get what they want! And when they do get what they *think* they want, Joan Crawford, grand mistress of the deadly dildo, makes goddamn sure it ain't what they expected!"

Jean stared worshipfully at Joan for a moment and Joan began to laugh. Stupendously pleased with herself, she poured another drink, took a swallow, turned almost happily to Jean.

"How about this?" Joan grandly cleared her throat. The lights dimmed and her faithful little spotlight-from-nowhere returned as Joan became a proud but very concerned mother, beseeching her errant daughter:

"Veda, darling!" she cried, wringing her jeweled fingers, "Everything I've ever done has been for you and you alone. I have sacrificed all I ever desired upon the alter of your malicious vanity! Now you say you're leaving me! Leaving your devoted mother, the only human being in this cold, savage world who will ever love you with that fierce, selfless love that only a mother can give!"

Joan took a magnificent drag at her cigarette and continued with soul-shaking sorrow. "How dare you run away with the only man I have ever loved!"

Joan now miraculously became this selfish, wilful daughter:

"I am sick of your martyrdom, mother! Sick of your martyrdom and sick of you! True, they say I'm spoiled, demanding and a snob but they don't live with you, mother!" sneered Joan as the daughter, "You fancy yourself a saint but you're nothing but a common washerwoman from the wrong side of the tracks and I melt with shame just to be seen on the street with you!"

Jean was entranced. The lights, somehow, again came up. Joan glowed, poured herself another drink, sat beside Jean, lit another cigarette, offered one to Jean who, dabbing her eyes, shook her head and exclaimed "Oh, Miss Crawford! That was wonnnderful!"

"So we have been told," whispered Joan, at last adrift in pleasure. Her romp down Memory Lane was finally proceeding with promise toward its doleful end. "An exceptionally great moment," she added. "For which I won an Oscar. I've many very great moments under my belt, darling," said Joan.

"So we have been told," mimicked Jean and began to laugh. Joan caught on, couldn't stop herself. The women clung together and roared with laughter. The bible Joan had been holding, fell to the floor.

"I almost like you, Harlow. You remind me of me," laughed Joan.

Jean bent, picked up the bible and handed it to her, said "Where'd you get this, Joanie? I never knew you was religious."

Joan instantly became the leering slattern, Sadie, "Me? Religious?!"

Joan sashayed across the room, dropped the bible on a chair, swivelled her hips and said "Honey, when I need religion I jist screw a preacher -- and," said Joan, giving her hips another hefty turn, "when I'm feeling exceptionally religious, I screw two, en brochette!"

Jean, giggling, undulated precisely as had Joan -- across the room to her. They clung together then collapsed on the sofa.

"Now you do it," said Joan, wiping the tears of raucous laughter from her eyes.

"Do what?" said Jean, carefully combing her still damp, platinum curls.

"Act."

"Act?"

"Act, for chrissake!" said Joan, "You've just had a lesson from Crawford. I wasn't doing it for my health, Harlow. I'm doing you a favor."

"Now? Act now?" whimpered Jean.

"Yeah. Now! Act -- as in *actress*!"

"But I ain't got no director."

"I'll be your director."

"No. My makeup ain't right. I ain't got no script," pleaded Jean.

"Just do as I say. Don't be a goddamned coward."

"I ain't no coward!"

"You ain't no actress neither."

"I *am* a actress!"

Joan moved briskly to one of her suitcases, threw it open and snatched out a fringed, red satin dress. She tossed it to Jean.

"Show me you're an actress, Harlow! Show me what you can do!"

Jean froze, petrified by the thought of acting for the mighty Joan Crawford.

"Put on the damned dress, Miss Jean Harlow!" commanded Joan.

Jean slipped out of the negligee, pulled on the red dress, turned her back to Joan, said "Button me."

"If you're really an actress, Harlow," said Joan, buttoning the back of Jean's dress, "you'll feel different already. Do you feel different?"

"Yeah, I guess so."

"How different?" demanded Joan.

"A little different," said Jean.

"A little?!" cried Joan.

"Yeah, a *little!*" yelled Jean.

"When an actress changes clothes she should feel it in her guts!" screamed Joan, "Take it off!"

"But I just put the fucker on!"

"Take it off," said Joan, calmer, and unbuttoned the red dress. Jean stepped out of it and, nude, waited.

"You aren't ready for red yet," said Joan. "Put on the white negligee again. I need innocence."

"You can say that again," grumbled Jean to herself, and slipped on the negligee.

"Stand over there!"

Jean walked obediently to the balcony doors.

"You're Lucille LeSueur," said Joan.

"I'm you?"

"Not me *now,*" snapped Joan. "Me *then.* Your latest father's just run off and deserted your family. Cry!"

Jean began to laugh. Joan rushed at her, shook her.

"Cry, damn you! Your father's just left you and your mother and brother! Cry!"

Jean pulled away. "Leave me alone!"

"That's it!"

"Damn you, Crawford! Who the hell do you think you are, pushing me around?!"

"That's it!" said Joan. "That's it! You're talking to my -- your mother! Cry now, damn it! Cry your damned eyes out!"

Jean was so angry she began to cry.

Joan raced to the tiny bathroom, grabbed a scrub brush, returned and thrust it into Jean's hand.

"You monster!" yelled sobbing Jean.

"Get on your knees, Harlow!"

Jean shook her head, refused and Joan charged in, forced her to the floor, cried "Scrub! You're scrubbing floors in a convent school. Lucille scrubbed floors to support herself. The nuns turned their heads and the girls spat on her. Scrub now, lowlife! Scrub those goddamned floors till they are as immaculate as the holy order that fouled 'em!"

Joan grabbed Jean's arm, violently thrust it back and forth. "Scrub!" she shouted, "Scrub like your tiny life depended on it! Because it does!"

Jean scrubbed. Joan lit another cigarette, puffed furiously and hovered over Jean who glared up at her.

"That's right," said Joan. "That's so right. There's hope for you yet, Harlow. Now listen. Your mother marries again, see? A Mr Cassin. And Mr Cassin calls you 'Billy' because you're a tomboy. So you're now Billy Cassin. You like your new Dad. A lot. Maybe too much. So your mother throws you out. React!"

Jean was exhausted, sat frowning but attentive as Joan abruptly began to play her own mother: "I seen you lookin' at

Mr Cassin, Billy, and it's high time you got the hell out! There's people in this wide, wide world who might appreciate that slinky ass o' yours. But I ain't one of 'em! So beat it! Clear off! Did you hear me?! Keep your grimy fingers offa Mr Cassin and get outta my house!"

Jean shrank away on her knees as Joan's wild-eyed 'Mrs Cassin' bore down on her but Joan suddenly stopped, turned sharply from the intimidated Jean and poured herself another drink. She returned to stand swaying over Jean whose awe had morphed to anger. "Damn you!" screamed Jean with all the strength she could muster, "I'm a goddamned movie star too!"

"Get up!" yelled Joan. "And prove it!"

Jean was obstinate, crouched on the floor gripping her knees and glowering her own sensational close-up, a frightening, forty-foot frown. Joan launched herself at Jean, grabbed her under the arms and ferociously heaved her up. Jean fought for a moment but acquiesced as she saw Joan shapeshift, become yet another former self, the young Billy Cassin. It was common knowledge in Hollywood that Joan had at one time used the name of her mother's second husband whom she adored.

Joan's voice became slangy. Her body proposed the rawest sex, reeked of it. Jean's anger melted into fascination. Yet again she could not take her eyes from Joan.

"You're touring, Billy, with this vaudeville troupe, see?"

"I ain't Billy! I am Miss Jean Harlow, Hollywood star!"

"You're who I say you are, Harlow. You're playing Billy Cassin and I'm the goddamned director in this fucking story!"

Jean sneered, "You must be dreamin'!"

Joan rushed closer, slapped Jean's face, screamed, "You are Billy Cassin and you're in an act with three other dames!"

Jean was scared, backed down. This crazy lady who thought she was Crawford was as nutty as her Aunt Dot's fruitcake! And she had a gun. "Okay, okay," said Jean. "Okay."

"You're a dame, got that?" said Joan, "A dame. Not a lady. So don't go gettin' no ideas. That comes later. Now, listen. These three other dames have saved all their money, see? Snuffled it all away in itsy-bitsy piggy-banks and bought six flashy dresses for their act."

Joan snatched up the red dress again, threw it at Jean, yelled "Put it on!"

"Just who the hell do you think you are?!" cried Jean.

"Put on the dress, Billy. You stole it. Put on the goddamned dress!" roared Joan.

Jean threw off the innocent white negligee, pulled on the flapper-fringed, red satin dress as Joan, more tenderly than she'd meant to, assisted.

"Billy didn't have nothin' of her own, see?" continued Joan as young Billy Cassin. "She needed to get somewhere. But you don't get nowhere with nothin'. You need somethin' to get somewhere, see? Somethin' nice on your back."

Joan buttoned up Jean's back. The dress fit perfectly, as though created by Metro Wardrobe for Jean Harlow alone. Or was this simply a fevered figment of Joan's tipsy imagination? She'd had several odd spells lately, was worried...but this was *her* romp, *her* illustrious past, *her* own private Memory Lane! On she went:

"So Billy steals them dresses, every damned one of 'em!" said Joan-as-Billy. "And she has to take off quick and she sees this man..."

Jean was now in costume. Joan pushed her forward into a spotlight that came from nowhere but was not to be questioned -- by either of them. "So act!" demanded Joan the director, as she relinquished centre-stage to Jean.

Jean smiled uncertainly.

"I SAID ACT!" yelled Joan. "He looks like he's got bucks. Lotsa bucks. Maybe he's rich. He sure as hell's got influence 'cause he owns the theatre you're gonna dance in tonight. He's lookin' at you, Billy. Right now. Smile Billy!"

Jean grinned hesitantly.

"That's a smile?!" cried Joan. Jee-sus! I've seen sweeter smiles on a horse's ass! I want an if-you-put-me-in-the-first -line-of-the-chorus-so's-everybody'll-see-me-then-I'll-screw -you smile! Let's have it, little Miss Jeanie Harlow! Show your stuff! SMILE!"

Jean, a wholly intuitive actress, clearly felt the rush of Joan's description and began to glow with its possibilities. It felt important and she loved to feel important. Her smile was a spectacular beginning and she knew it. It filled the room like lightning. She had imagined it on a huge, glorious movie screen. It worked every darn time!

Joan was impressed. "Wonderful, honey! You've been there yourself, haven't you? He's standin' in the wings at the final rehearsal and you're kickin' high. Kickin' your young heart out in the second line of the chorus. But he's gotta put you in the first line! Middle-girl in the first line!"

Jean managed a high chorus-line-kick.

"But you jist got to be up front! So smile, Billy Cassin! Smile!" cried the elated Joan as she danced in place, reliving every crazy second.

Jean kicked high, smiled another tempestuous smile that radiated health and beauty, and was irresistible.

"Not bad. Not bad at all, we'll make a star of you yet."

"I am a star! I am a goddamned international movie star!" shrieked Jean.

Joan was ecstatic. "That's right, Billy! You tell 'em, baby!" She smashed out her cigarette in the coconut shaped ashtray, rushed to furious Jean, embraced her passionately. Jean struggled, broke away, screamed "I ain't Billy!"

Joan glared at her, said "Feel your belly, Billy."

"I ain't Billy! I am Jean Harlow, a international, darned movie star!"

Joan became Billy Cassin again, her language slid from Crawford's rigorous diction into an angry street slur.

"Go ahead. Feel yer belly, Billy Cassin. It's gettin' bigger. Somebody left his callin' card."

Jean unconsciously felt her stomach.

"Think, Billy. Who was it, done the dirt on you? It couldn't have been Mr Chorus-line 'cause his tubes was tied."

Jean pondered broadly, camera-ready, smooth brow now severely creased beneath her radiant tangle of luminous curls.

"Least he said his tubes was tied," offered Joan-as-Billy. "Least that's what the sonofabitch said when he refused to help you, to assist a poor girl in trouble, Billy. When he fired you on the spot!"

Lightning split the black, windswept sky and rain came, suddenly, in great battering sheets. Jean was angry, hurtled to the balcony doors, screamed "Don't it never stop?!"

Joan ran to her and drew impossible Jean back into the impossible spotlight. "Concentrate, Billy Cassin! So you packed up your stolen dresses, didn't you? You got outta town fast -- that evil bastard sicced his mugs on you, threatened to fix your face. He didn't want you all pregnant and pathetic, hangin' around crampin' his style, did he?"

Joan-Billy became Joan again, took a swallow from her tall glass and a drag at her cigarette, said "What do you do now, Missy actress"?

Jean became 'Billy', determined and defiant. "I get a abortion!" she cried.

"Sure you get an abortion, stupid," said Joan. "But first you need money. Lots of it. You gotta get a job. So with them stolen dresses in your cardboard suitcase you start to pound the pavement. Let's see it, baby!"

Joan grabbed one of her suitcases, slid it across the floor to Jean. Jean picked it up, walked a few steps, set it down. Joan was suddenly Billy again, said "Jesus! You look like you jist stepped outta your satin sheets into your goddamned bubble bath. Remember, Billy, you're tired and broken. It's the Great Depression, for God's sake! You gotta eat! You been sleepin' in alleys and doin' a little business there on the side. *Look* like it!"

Jean sagged. Sad and broken, she picked up the suitcase, managed a feeble step. Joan took a deep, satisfying drag at her cigarette, delighting in Jean's misery. She enjoyed forcing Jean to suffer as she, Lucille-Billy-Joan had. Someone had to suffer for her suffering. Who could be better than the spoiled Jean Harlow who never did a decent day's work in her life.

So Joan-Billy, as director, went on: "Then you get lucky, honey. Some boozy bastard hires you at the My Blue Heaven Ballroom because you give his moth-eaten Moll one of your fine, stolen dresses. You're a dance hostess now. Jerk-offs buy tickets to sample your charms on the dance floor. The horny bastards ruin one of those flashy dresses of yours before you wise up and wear a cheap, washable, apron. And what you do, Billy, on your own time is your own business. And I ain't talkin' takin' in laundry. You need more money, Billy, and pronto, 'cause abortions don't come in a box of cornflakes. Feel your belly, Billy."

Jean frowned and felt her stomach again, looked suitably frightened.

"Whose tiny bastard have you got in there, young Miss Billy Cassin? You sure it's Mr Chorus-line's? Or is it that waiter you screwed in the men's washroom for his Sunday afternoon's tips?"

Jean shook her head.

"Know the feelin'?" coached Joan, "Been there, done that?"

Jean stubbornly refused to answer. Joan ignored this and quaffed the rest of her drink, staggered a bit but said, almost tenderly, "Not to worry, honey. Your tiny bastard will never see the light of day. Sit down."

Jean would show this so called superstar, Crawford! She began to emote at full throttle. She dropped herself, writhing with worry, to the shabby sofa. She waved her arms, pleaded with the sky and the front row seats of some unseen movie theatre. She ostentatiously began to wipe her eyes, secretly searching from the corner of one, for her tardy film crew. Where the heck were they?

"Ever seen an illegal abortionist's waiting room?" asked Joan.

After an amazingly comprehensive range of expressions, Jean settled on two: demoralized and confused. And hesitantly nodded.

Joan was pleased, continued, "One thing they don't have at a back-alley abortionist's is magazines. One thing they do have is cockroaches. That's right, baby," grinned Joan-as-Billy as she saw the revulsion on Jean's face. "You're waitin' there in this back-alley butcher's waitin' room and a door opens and this young girl, she can't be no more than fourteen...this young girl comes out holdin' her belly and there's a slush of mascara and tears all over her empty little face and there's blood on her skirt and the skirt's back-to-front but she don't care about nothin'. As she staggers out she leaves a trail of tiny specks of blood that follow her out the door like the bread-crumbs that Hansel and Gretel, in that fairy tale, scattered to find their way back. But there ain't no way back for this bloody child who will die in the dark alley just outside. This child ain't no Gretel. And this ain't no Fairy Tale. Spread your legs, Harlow!"

Jean gasped, hesitated.

"Spread your legs, Billy Cassin!" commanded Joan.

Jean obediently spread her legs.

Joan became herself again -- the elegant gesture with her cigarette, the way she held her glass of vodka and crossed her still gorgeous legs -- it was all there, and she knew it. The pin-spot was again hers alone and she was perfect. That forty-foot movie screen contained no one but Joan Crawford as she whispered: "I lay there with my dress up to my chin. He looked down at me, grinned for a moment. I was glad it wasn't longer. He went to wash that child's blood from his hands and I thanked God for little favors -- he was at least washing his hands before he touched me. I looked around and I couldn't see the forest for the forceps...and the prongs and the knives and the little pincers and the big pincers and the scissors and the tiny, tiny, so very tiny hooked something-or-others that lay about that butcher's shop. LEGS WIDER, HARLOW!"

Jean was terrified but complied.

"Get ready!"

Jean squinched her eyes in horror. Joan grabbed a wire coat-hanger from her steamer trunk and twisted it till it became a long tool with a small hook at one end. Jean was oblivious, lost in terrified imaginings. She lay, eyes shut, legs spread, unseemly but somehow still ravishing on the gaudy, bamboo-legged sofa.

Her face now mysteriously shadowed in a hooded black raincoat, Joan became a grotesque mock of the illegal abortionist. With her drink in one hand and the hooked wire held like a sword before her, she stood swaying over Jean. Suddenly, Joan bent, thrust her glass at Jean, said "Take a swallow, baby, you'll need it."

Jean took a swallow. She needed it.

"This illegal back-alley abortionist, this spurious doctor," hissed Joan, "this butcher, gives you a slug of gin from a dirty glass, pours a little more, drinks it himself then soaks his bloody hanky in it, and rubs it on his long, hooked wire. This man, this cruel but necessary criminal, was our only resort when a woman was poor and abortion was against the law."

Joan poured vodka over her fine, silk handkerchief, wiped the hooked hanger wire, and now, as the illegal abortionist's terrifying stand-in, sprang at Jean who screamed and rolled aside, sobbing hysterically.

Joan threw down the twisted wire, threw off the hooded raincoat and hugged Jean, cuddled and consoled her as Jean sobbed "Mama! Mama!"

"Mama's here, baby. Mama's here, baby Jean," whispered Joan.

Jean became a small child clutching at Joan who gently, slowly, rocked her back and forth.

"Mama's here, Jeanie, Mama's here."

Joan freed one arm from her comforting embrace, poured another vodka, took a long swallow, gave Jean a sip, whispered "Better, darling?"

In the tiniest of voices, Jean managed "Yeah."

"That wasn't all that happened to Billy Cassin," said Joan

"To *you*," whispered Jean's plaintive, baby's voice, terrified of more horror to come.

Joan took a cigarette from her gold case, lit it, and captured the imagination of a million absent people. "To me and Billy," she repeated, "That wasn't all the happened."

"Please, Joanie," said Jean's tiny, baby voice. "Spare me the dee-tails. Please."

But Joan wasn't listening, she was Billy again, said "Billy Cassin's belly got bigger and bigger when it shoulda got smaller and smaller. Bigger and bigger 'stead of smaller and smaller. She thought it was a inflammation or somethin'."

"A inflammation?" asked Jean.

"Uh-huh," mimed Joan-as-Billy. "Or somethin'. A lot of lonely bleedin' was on her agenda."

"You bled a lot?"

"That's what I said, ain't it?! Then one fine morning a few months later I wake up in this cheap hotel on a real bloody bed, see? With this little thing beside me. I ain't quite awake so I don't know what the hell it is. But it moves and it looks at me with big, cloudy eyes and do you know what I say?"

Jean shook her head.

"I say," announced Joan, "I say *What the hell is this?!* It is attached to an umbilical cord thingy that trails right up into my..."

"Jeez! The abortion didn't..."

Joan became Joan again, said "I lifted the bedclothes to get a better look. I was foolishly curious in those days. The little thing...it was...unformed, made tiny noises, tiny, jerky moans. I pulled it next to me and it snuffled and made the tiny noises again. I put what might have been, should have been, its mouth, on my nipple but it didn't suck. Its mouth wasn't, didn't seem to be, developed enough to suck. I hugged it for awhile. Till it stopped breathing and it turned blue and it felt cold. Then I cut it free with my manicure scissors and I put it in a paper bag and I threw it away. That's what millions of women did when abortion was illegal. I was lucky. Thousands of others died."

Jean tore herself from Joan and leapt up with a hand over her mouth and rushed to the bathroom and vomited.

Joan rose, unsteadily. She might have sobbed like an ordinary person, like some shop assistant, but she didn't. She was Joan Crawford. It helped a helluva lot being Joan Crawford. Or was it Lucille LeSueur or was it Billy Cassin? "You pays yer money and you gets yer choice," whispered Joan -- as Joan.

She was forty feet tall again as she poured herself another drink. Oddly, she did not feel drunk but only alarmingly blasé as she drew a cigarette from her gold case, lit it and took a drag. No one seemed to enjoy a cigarette as much as Joan who stood at the balcony door exulting in the torrential rain, distant thunder, and Jean's violent retching behind the dingy little bathroom door.

Jean slept soundly in the white negligee, its high-ruffled collar softly framing her flawless face and Joan bent warily over her, concerned, longing, even motherly. But after a camera-conscious, seriously vigilant moment she was again at her little rattan dressing table mirror.

In the eerie light of a small lamp with a palm-frond shade, Joan began, in bra and panties, to apply makeup. She shadowed her eyes deep sea-green, penciled her eyebrows from stark to severe, and applied heavy, black mascara. She rouged each cheek an unnerving scarlet, and formed with heavy lipstick and practiced fingers, her trademark, cinematically-certain mouth. As she worked, her face took on her Sadie slattern look. Each small gesture became more exaggerated and offhand -- an unmistakable invitation to pleasure, and through that pleasure, doom. Just as her script had ordered.

As she rose, Joan cast a confident smile at her mirror and snatched her red satin Sadie dress from the floor where Jean had thrown it. Joan sniffed the dress. It was fortunately free of Jean's sick. Joan slipped it on and buttoned its back easily and expertly -- who needed Metro's Wardrobe department to do things she'd been forced to do for herself since she was a small child? She twirled and struck a pose and now regarded her Sadie reflection in a full-length bamboo-framed mirror that emerged from nowhere. Joan never questioned such good fortune which was, she always felt, her due for the many sacrifices she'd made for World Fame. These were her exact thoughts as she turned from the full-length mirror and strolled provocatively to the balcony doors and peered, this time as Sadie would, into the rain and screamed, "Don't it never stop?!"

Sadie-Joan wandered from lamp to lamp, tilting their shades to her advantage and again found herself drawn to, and pausing over, the lovely, sleeping Jean. She bent to stroke Jean's cheek but drew back, terrified she could be mortally wounded by such beauty. It wasn't time. Not quite time to be mortal.

Joan was surprised when she found the tiny revolver in her hand. The Prop Man must have put it there. She knew what she must do. She'd known it all along. She kneeled beside Jean and placed the revolver at Jean's temple, cocked it, held it there as Jean sighed, turned and moaned in her sleep.

"Who are you?" spat Sadie-Joan. "Why the hell did you come here?! I want the truth, see?!"

Jean whimpered. Joan withdrew the revolver, laid it on the

sofa table, took a cigarette from a crumpled pack -- no gold cigarette cases for Sadie! She lit the cigarette with a lowly match and exhaled harshly, nothing like the elegant Joan's nicotine shtick. Sadie Joan once again gazed down at the sleeping golden girl and dropped herself gracelessly into a chair and puffed fiercely on her cigarette, the tiny revolver at her elbow. Gone was the studied elegance of Crawford who now enjoyably and dangerously inhabited the primitive tramp called Sadie.

An unearthly aura hovered above the sleeping Jean who sighed again, moaned again and twisted restlessly on the sofa and woke and sat up. Her face glistened in the unearthly light. "I am God's perfect child," she whispered. "I am his golden angel."

"I was God's perfect child," whispered Joan from her chair. "I was his golden angel."

Jean glided to her phonograph, switched it on. It began to play its slow, low-down jazz. She swayed magnificently with the music, whispered "My body is a temple."

"My body was a temple," echoed Joan, who crouched miserably in her chair.

"I have clean habits and pure, uplifting thoughts," whispered Jean.

"Me too," whispered Joan.

"I am as chaste as any girl in Hollywood has a right to be in these Great Depression years."

"I was as chaste as any *ambitious* girl in Hollywood had a right to be in those Great Depression years," whispered Joan.

"I am a international star," whispered Jean, moving gracefully, confidently, with the music.

Joan rose from her chair and joined Jean in the circle of impossible light. She began to sway with Jean as they danced to the haunting rhythms of their solemn words.

"I am an international star," whispered Joan.

"My Mama says I was sent to earth to bring happiness to

mortals," said Jean. "I am famous for my platinum blonde hair and my ethereal beauty as well as for my full breasts and my pungent sense of humor. I am the Blonde Bombshell of the whole, darned world."

"My parasite mother and no-good brother showed up on my swanky Hollywood doorstep one day," said Joan. "I swallowed my pride and tolerated their insults and ingratitude and vulgar behavior. I supported them in style till the day they died. They never thanked me."

"Every rung up my *glittering ladder of success* was directed by my dear Mama and applauded by millions. They wept when I was widowed by suicide at age twenty-two and they rejoiced when I recovered a month later to climb to new heights of movie glory."

The women clasped hands and began to close-dance.

"I never had to worry about nothin'," said Jean. "Mama and my Step-Daddy took care of my money. Oh boy! did they take care of my money! I am God's and Mama's perfect child."

"I was a trusting child," said Joan. "I was pretty. I washed and ironed my own clothes. I always had ribbons in my hair. I stole them. White ones. I was a trusting child. It did not pay."

"My Step-Daddy and Mama had good sex. Step-Daddy's grunts and Mama's shouts in the night excited me," said Jean. "I decided it was better for me to live alone so I moved out. My Step-Daddy was too attractive. It worried me 'cause I am a good girl, I am."

"Good girls got nowhere in the thirties," snapped Joan. "The economy was shit. You were either born with money or you made it on your back."

"White is my favorite color," whispered Jean. "Radiant, in white, I am irresistible."

"I had to work hard," said Joan. "All on my own. I kicked ass and crushed balls. Made friends, lost 'em. My heart was broken more than once but I went back for more. Got it. Then gave as good as I got! Marilyn Monroe was a piker compared to Joan Crawford!"

"I love world premieres!" cried Jean.

"Me too!" cried Joan.

"I love the red carpet treatment," sighed Jean. "I jist love the feel of my nipples against my tight, low cut, shimmering dresses and black-plumed, white ermines. I love the jewels. I love the oh's and ah's of the crowd and their breath like hot summer wind on my bare, creamy-white shoulders."

"I love to be so close and yet so very far away," sighed Joan. "I love to hear the screams of people who want me but cannot have me. It helps me forget where I came from."

"I came from nowhere and got somewhere fast," said Jean.

"You've got to be fast to get somewhere," laughed Joan, and with a great, ear-piercing scratch, she jerked the tone arm from Jean's record, and stood angrily facing her. Blinding lightning flashed and thunder crashed, mimicking Joan's fury. Torrents of rain pounded instantly after and Jean rushed to the balcony doors, cried "Jee-sus, don't it never stop rainin' around here?! It gives me the willies!"

The pounding of rain came up ever louder. Again, on cue. Expert cues and mysterious lightning were not to be questioned tonight in a shabby little room entangled in an unknowable strand of time.

Joan tenderly took her hand and drew Jean back from the balcony. Jean, anxious for a moment, touched a stray platinum curl on her smooth, ever-photogenic brow. She brushed it with her lovely, pink-nailed finger to where it ought to be, summoned a surfeit of emotion, said, "I miss my Mama. My Mama says we're perfect, all of us but that I am more perfect than most."

Joan poured a small drink for Jean, handed it to her and they sat. "Have a perfect slug of gin, wonder-child."

Jean took the glass, drained it in an instant, said "A perfect child of God don't drink. But I do. Sometimes when I'm bad. When I'm bad Mama taught me how to pray and I say: dear

God, I am so sorry I been bad."

"What?!" cried Joan.

"Mama says I make God sad when I am bad."

"Make God sad?! Jee-sus Christ!"

"Him too. Plus the Holy Ghost. The three of 'em," said Jean.

"Do you really think God cares about a cheap, amoral little tramp like you? Mary Magdalene, you ain't! Don't trivialize God! You might need him one day! Even us movie stars know that!"

"I didn't ask for fame! It just come to me," protested Jean with a winning smile.

"Christ! Another Hollywood martyr!" exclaimed Joan. "I'm sick of 'em! I worked my balls off to get where I am and I loved it!"

"Lotsa people been wonderin', Joanie, whatever happened to them balls of yours."

"I chewed 'em off, honey, and I stuffed 'em in my bra." Joan laughed. "How's your belly?"

"So-so. I ain't got a epidemic if that's what you're thinkin', Joanie."

"Why not? You probably screwed the whole crew on your ship."

""The bible says don't judge others by yourself, honey. Besides, Disease don't enter the temple of us perfect beings."

"Come off it, God's perfect child. That temple of yours is entered regularly, sweetheart, and not to pray. So don't go puttin' on airs with Sadie."

The pounding noise of rain again filled the room. Jean sat up sharply, rose and began to pace with artfully timed turns and returns synched perfectly with monumentally arched eyebrows.

"Can't somebody stop the rain?! It's drivin' me..."

"Ask the director, Harlow," snapped Joan. "But first, tell me, why did you come here?"

"On and on. The rain. It goes on and on. Don't it never stop?

Don't it?!"

"Why did you come here?!" demanded Joan.

"Jesus! I told ya!" said Jean, pulling the negligee closer around her to accentuate her sensational body beneath chiffon that was, to her delight, now virtually transparent. "Do we have to go through that again?!"

"Young missy!" cried a voice at the door.

"Yeah?" shouted Joan.

"Young missy!"

"That'd be me, Joanie," said Jean, "Yes?!"

"We find young missy's suitcase! It by your door, young missy! Me no come close! Everybody real sick! Bye-bye!"

Jean stopped pacing and strode to the door.

"Wait!," cried Joan, and was beside Jean in an instant, the spray-can of disinfectant in her hand.

Jean, directed by Joan, opened the door. Joan covered her nose and mouth with a hanky, leaned out, sprayed the suitcase and nodded to Jean who carried it in and, as directed by Joan, set it on a small bamboo table and opened it. A filmscript fell out and Joan snatched it away, retreated to the sofa to read it.

"Hey, gimmee my script!" yelled Jean. "I gotta learn it by tomorrow!"

Joan ignored her, continued reading.

"Hey! Gimmee that back!"

Joan looked up in horror, screamed "Sadie! What the fuck is this?! *You* as Sadie?!"

"Honey, I been tryin' to tell you that all night. I'm replacin' you. Got that? I am playin' Sadie in this movie and I gotta learn my lines by tomorrow morning so give me back my darned script!"

"But I was Sadie. Forty-five years ago. In '32."

"Whaddaya mean?! This is 1932! What are you? Some kinda crazy broad? I don't even think you're Crawford! She's nuts but she ain't a screwball like you! You don't even look like Crawford. You're too goddamned old to be Crawford. Jeez, you must be seventy or somethin'! Crawford's about my age, give or take a few years. Who are *you*?"

"I am Joan Crawford and the year, my dear, whoever the hell *you* are, is 1977!"

"Then your a goner, Joanie. 'Cause your gonna die in '77!"

"How the hell do you know?!" Joan threw down the filmscript, rushed to the pile of Jean's clothes on the bed and grabbed a red dress from it, tossed it at Jean.

"What the heck?" said Jean. "Are we playin' musical wardrobes again?"

"Just put on the damned dress! We'll see who plays Sadie in my film!"

"My film!" screamed Jean.

"Put on the dress! We'll see whose film this is!!"

Jean threw the red dress into Joan's face. Joan threw it back. Jean threw it back at Joan who stormed over and ripped off Jean's white negligee.

The naked Jean, rushed to find clothes in her own suitcase but Joan grabbed it from her and threw it across the room scattering the fine clothes everywhere. Jean stumbled hysterically around the room to find something to wear but Joan tripped her, pushed her to the floor and sat on her, brutally holding her down.

"You let me up, you horsey bitch!" screamed Jean.

Joan slapped her face but lost her balance as Jean suddenly rolled aside, throwing Joan to the floor. Clutching and screaming at one another, they rolled over and over across the floor until Jean got away, ran to the balcony and cried, "Help! Help! That horsey bitch is gonna moider me!"

Joan pulled herself up from the floor and sprang onto the balcony, grabbed Jean. Lightning flashed and thunder crashed -- right on cue again -- and the rain came in ever greater torrents as the two frantic women struggled ever more cinematically.

Jean broke away again and ran back into the room. Joan

was at her heels and snatched the tiny, pearl handled revolver from the dressing table before Jean could reach it. Jean froze as Joan aimed the gun at her and again tossed the red dress in Jean's face and cried "Put it on! Put it on and we'll be twins!"

Joan kept careful aim as Jean obediently put on the dress. The rain pounded the low tin roof in great thrashing torrents and Jean screamed, "Make it stop! Make the rain stop!"

"That's it, Sadie! You're crazy from the rain and you're converted! You want to pay for your sins. You can't wait to get back to Frisco and do time in the pen for petty theft. Go to your phonograph."

Jean obeyed, switched on the small wind-up phonograph.

"Not now, dummy! Don't listen now to it now. Get into your part! A converted whore doesn't listen to the music of sin. That would be goin' back to her old ways, wouldn't it? Just look at it for a minute, think about the music and how you'd love to hear it again but it's evil. That kind of music on that infernal machine is evil -- that's what the crazy preacher called it, an infernal machine, didn't he? And here he is now! Bangin' on your door! Listen, Sadie! Listen to him bangin' on your door!"

Joan, in her identical red satin dress, knocked on a wall with an empty vodka bottle, cried "Pray, Sadie! Pray!"

Jean's face broke with fear -- perfect for her close-up. She prayed a camera lurked somewhere near or all this bother would be one terrifying waste.

"What could he want at this hour of the night?" said Joan. "Don't just stand there, cringe against that rattan wall."

Jean shrank appropriately against the wall, anguished eyes still searching for that darn camera. Where was it?!

"You better let him in, Sadie, see what he wants."

Jean pretended to open a door.

"Look at his eyes, Sadie. What do you see there?"

"Dee-sire!" whimpered Jean. "I see dee-sire!"

"What do you feel, Sadie?"

"Chaste!"

"How do you spell it?" said Jean

"With a T! I'm a good girl, I am! I don't wanna do that no more!"

"Not even for ready money?" said Joan. "It's the Great Depression, honey!"

"Not even for ready money! Not never, not no-how!"

"Then scream," said Joan. "Scream your converted whore's heart out! Scream so you can feel it to the tips of your toes!"

Jean screamed, and she could feel it to the tips of her toes.

"Now, wobble a little and faint!!

"No, Joanie, Sadie wouldn't faint!" said Jean.

"She would now. She's converted! Bad women fuck but good women faint. That's the golden rule of Hollywood." Joan aimed the revolver at Jean. "I said FAINT!"

Jean fainted and fell on the sofa.

"Not on the sofa, for chrissake!" yelled Joan. "Fall on the floor. Get real!"

"I am real, Joan Crawford!" cried Jean. "More real than you will ever be!"

"We'll see who's real or not! Fall...on...the floor or I'll blow your bloody brains out!"

Jean tumbled from the sofa to the floor.

"Here is where the camera cuts away," said Joan, "and the lights go out as our crazy preacher friend has his evil way with you. The next thing we know is this loony preacher sonofabitch feels so damned guilty he has run out and shot himself. But you are changed! Get up, show me how you've changed!"

"Of course I'm changed! I know I've changed! I've read my darned script ain't I?!"

"Then act changed!" cried Joan. "Now is the time to turn on your phonograph and react. You've just been raped! You don't believe in nothin' no more! You're disillusioned!"

Jean slowly raised herself from the floor and carefully rearranged her breasts to their fullest advantage in the low-cut red dress. Joan glanced at her own breasts, winced. She watched Jean enviously as she slouch-walked to the phonograph, gave the crank a few turns and switched it on and undulated to the soft, low-down jazz.

"Not too bad. You just might be up to it."

"Whaddaya mean *might*?! I *am* up to it!" yelled Jean. "Cause I am a actress!"

"C'mere," said Joan, motioning with the little revolver. Jean hesitated.

"C'mere, I said!"

Jean approached fearfully. She had no idea what this crazy hag who called herself Crawford might do. But Jean had become sleepy, felt herself sliding into something odd, some half-awake stupor. Where on the set was her canvas movie star chair? She needed to rest. Her will was declining. She was too vulnerable. Was this her director's mistake? Or hers? And who the hell was her director? My God! It was Joan! Crawford was her director!

"We're gonna gamble for the part, Harlow. If you play Sadie it will be over my dead body."

Joan clicked open the chamber of the revolver, shook out all the bullets but one, clicked the chamber closed and spun it.

"We got a deal, Harlow?"

Jean slowly nodded yes. The women stood facing one another; one, dazed, one, mercilessly driven. Lightning flashed and close thunder crackled as Joan handed the tiny pearl handled revolver with one bullet in its chamber to Harlow. The rain pounded harder. Lightning transformed the room -- the technical crew was doing their stuff! Jean became ever more golden, ever more desirable. "The rain," murmured Jean, as she numbly accepted the gun, "Don't it never stop?"

"It might, Harlow, for you. Try it and see."

Jean shuddered as she brought the gun to her temple and paused.

"Pull the trigger, Jeanie," commanded Joan. "You'll never

know if you don't try."

"I can't," whispered Jean as she squeezed the trigger. The revolver only clicked. Jean, in a trance, offered the gun to Joan who reluctantly took it, hesitated then brought it to her temple, squeezed the trigger. The gun clicked again. Joan let out her breath and handed the gun back to Jean.

"The rain. It's drivin' me..." said Jean. Joan watched impassively as Jean brought the gun to her head and again squeezed the trigger and again the revolver only clicked.

"Make the rain stop," whispered Jean as she put the tiny revolver in Joan's sweating palm.

Joan shakily placed the gun to her temple and pulled the trigger. It clicked once again. Joan handed the tiny revolver back to Jean, who was now an obedient puppet. The gun dangled at Jean's side. Joan lifted Jean's arm, pushed the gun to Jean's temple. Jean held it there, staring blankly out over the balcony into the hot, driving rain, a glamorous, golden robot, the Blonde Bombshell of the whole, darned world.

Joan backed warily away as Jean pulled the trigger.

Jean's blood spattered in a small, pink puff against the rattan-covered wall of this run-down little room in the tropics, a thousand miles from what she was accustomed. Death had came by the tiniest of guns, pearl handled and expensive, a plan that had been conceived by Joan for Joan herself. Similar in many ways to the tragic death of Jean's husband many years before in Hollywood -- a demise that had created headlines for months. No one remembered now, but they would. As Joan by her own hand would soon follow Jean. That was her plan. That was why she came here. She had not counted on this visit from Harlow but she would make the most of it.

Joan had screamed as Jean fell and Joan had slumped to her knees on the sea-grass matting. She might have sobbed but she didn't. No one was here to see her emote. She'd thought they might be here -- that film crew. But she had been wrong about a lot of things lately. It was worrying. Anyway, Joan Crawford sobbed only for film cameras -- and only when she felt like it. She took Jean's lifeless hand in hers and held it to her cheek briefly and dropped it. Then reconsidered, picked up the hand again, decided there was a scene here and goddamn it, she was the only one around to play it. So, film crew or not, she did:

"I kinda liked you, Harlow. You reminded me of myself a couple of hundred years ago. We coulda been friends. I didn't even wanna do this goddamned movie. I worked for Metro, see? And they loaned me out to another studio as punishment for my affair with Mr Clark Gable. I didn't know a soul at the other studio. They didn't even shoot the film in Pago-Pago! They shot it on Catalina Island, just off the coast of California. One dollar fifty cents from Hollywood on a ratty little ferry boat, the cheapskates! Jee-sus! I couldn't work with that bunch of stuck-up, Broadway stage actors. I needed support and love. I didn't get it. They looked down on me, the bastards! We're so much alike. We're the same lady, Jean Harlow, you and me."

Joan smiled her grimmest smile. Her fans would love that smile!

Joan Crawford's performance as Sadie Thompson became in time -- with the iconic film, 'Mildred Pierce', for which she received an Oscar -- one of her greatest triumphs.

Joan let go Jean's hand, lifted a fold of Jean's red satin dress, sighed, let it fall. The rain pounded louder for a moment. She took Jean's head in her hands, pressed it against her breast.

"Now I lay me down to sleep, I pray the Lord my soul to keep," whispered Joan into Jean's ear and gently laid her back on the sea-grass matting. Jean's head wasn't bloody. It was but the tiniest hole from the tiniest gun -- pearl handled, a revolver. Joan loved her little revolver -- the tiny gun was soon to become both her execution and her resurrection. She would live again in the headlines of the World Press.

Joan hoisted Jean's body from the floor and with great effort laid her on the mosquito-netted bed. She was followed in the darkened room by the return of her propitious pin-spot -- where did this delicious little spotlight come from? Had the film crew actually arrived? -- in secret? But where were they hiding? She had been wrong about a lot of things lately. It was worrying. Where was the fucking fun? Her rollicking ride down Memory Lane was again sliding off the rails.

Joan took a swallow of vodka, found Jean's filmscript on the floor and tossed it beside her body. She snatched a cigarette from her gold cigarette case, elegantly lit it with a match -- where was her fancy lighter? -- and puffed it to life in yet another glorious reprise of her renowned cigarette sorcery. All with a lowly match! From a goddamned matchbook, no less! She grinned engagingly, careful, by tilting her face to keep that little spotlight at a flattering angle -- a half-inch tilt in either direction could spell doom for an engaging grin. Had she copped that unique golden grin from Jean? It was an admission she would never publicly make.

Joan took a long, emotive drag on her cigarette. Emotive, for chrissake! -- it had to be! She had, just now, helped a woman shoot herself in the head and this woman, whoever the hell she was, was lying here, right beside her! This must somehow show in her, Joan Crawford's, face, but in a forty-foot high close-up it had to be obvious without appearing obvious. Those stuck-up stage actors she'd worked with on Catalina Island in '32 were obvious -- didn't know the first thing about the silver screen. Joan smiled at her own filmic superiority and exhaled sublimely. The smoke glowed in a halo around her head, taking light from that pin-spot toward which she had artfully blown it. Joan knew about smoke. And light. Smoke came from a cigarette. Light came from a pin-spot. But where this mysterious pin-spot came from was unknown. She'd been wrong about a lot of things lately. It was worrying.

Joan stubbed out her cigarette in the coconut shaped ashtray and retrieved her tiny revolver from where it had fallen and salvaged a few bullets from her bag. She placed them, for tomorrow, carefully on the bamboo night table and lay down beside the lifeless Jean and whispered "Now I lay me down to sleep. I pray the Lord my soul to keep. If I should die before I wake. I pray the Lord my soul to take."

There they were, in bed together at last, on this mosquito netted bed, that contentious filmscript between them. It was a superb camera-angle from directly above. A camera-crane's dream. Two women, almost as twins in their identical, red flapper-fringed Sadie dresses. But were they? They might easily have been, but as the crane took the camera higher, they seemed, somehow to merge, to become one. Only one red-dressed Sadie.

After a lingering moment on Joan's supremely resolute face, her mysterious pin-spot disappeared. Darkness. Cut!

***

Her assistant tiptoed softly across the luxurious bedroom to the enormous bed. She was careful not to disturb her employer, a late-sleeper. As was usual she silently replaced the empty bottles of vodka with full. She emptied the overflowing coconut shaped ashtray and refilled the always empty gold cigarette case. But most importantly, she made absolutely certain the tiny, pearl handled, fake revolver-cum-cigarette lighter was precisely where it should be, not more than one inch away from the cigarette case, on the bedside table. As ordered.

The assistant briskly opened the curtains, and her platinum blonde hair ignited as the room flooded with bright sunlight, revealing a breathtaking view of the New York City skyline. Turning from the glare, she saw an open filmscript. It was the same tattered filmscript her employer read time after time and even as she slept, her fingers were in the still open pages clutching to keep her place.

The assistant shook her head, smiled, and was drawn by a low hum and saw that the tape recorder was still on. Her employer, a famous actress, had the night before been recording notes for her autobiography.

But now it was time for a very late breakfast. Always one slice of extremely crisp, thoroughly drained bacon and, whether the sleeping actress was interested or not, a single poached egg on a very large dish. As she left, the assistant, who was a dish herself, pressed 'rewind' on the recorder. Before the assistant typed from the tape they would, as always, listen to it together when she returned with the breakfast tray and the daily rose in a crystal vase.

"Ms Crawford," whispered her assistant, upon her return. "Breakfast. The rain's finally stopped. It's a lovely, sunny day."

Ms Crawford always slept late, particularly after a bottle or two of vodka, and did not wake. This was usual. The beautiful blonde assistant smiled, set the tray on a small table and went to the tape recorder, switched on the play button. Perhaps Ms Crawford's own voice would wake her. She went back to the bed, whispered "Breakfast, Ms Crawford, but you'll have to put down your script. Here ma'am, let me take it for you."

The attractive assistant attempted to take the script from Joan, but Joan would not let go and her stiff body slumped forward, dead fingers defiantly gripping the script as though her life had depended upon it.

The assistant screamed and rushed from the room to call for help as Joan's voice, strong and determined spoke from the tape recorder:

> "...I played shopgirls too. Lots of 'em. Shopgirls from the other side of the tracks who made it big. Dimestore clerks in Omaha and Milwaukee and Boise, Idaho identified with me. If I could make it big so could they. I worked hard not to

disappoint them. I became a superstar. If you've worked hard and you're famous, be proud of it. I love to be recognized. When I hear people say, 'There goes Joan Crawford!' I turn and look them right in the eye and I say, Yeah! I'm Joan Crawford! How the hell are you doing?!"

www.ingramcontent.com/pod-product-compliance
Lightning Source LLC
Chambersburg PA
CBHW031333170626
46807CB00002B/675